RANGER TO THE RESCUE

TEXAS RANGER SERIES ~ BOOK 2

RENAE BRUMBAUGH GREEN

WILD HEART
BOOKS

ISBN-13: 978-1-942265-19-1

To Charis ~ May God give you all the desires of your heart.

CHAPTER 1

1881
HOUSTON, TEXAS

*A*melia Cooper checked her reflection in the glass shop window for the third time before heading up the street to where she knew Evan Covington might be locking up his office for the lunch hour. Not that she was trying to bump into him or anything.

Okay, so maybe she was trying to see him. But what was wrong with that? He was a professional acquaintance. Well, more than an acquaintance. More like a...a friend. After all, hadn't she helped free him from the gallows and clear his name when he'd been wrongly arrested as a ruthless killer?

Over the last couple of months, since he was set free, he'd set up a law office and drawn quite the business. So what in the world was wrong with her asking to interview him again, this time about his law practice? Readers were curious about what had become of the James Weston Hardy look-alike. And a story in the newspaper surely wouldn't hurt his business at all. Besides, it would give her a break from the endless society-page drivel Mr. Thomas insisted she write, day in and day out. Evan was no longer exactly a news story, but at least his story wouldn't contain a recipe or a new fashion trend.

Still, her heart beat a little faster in anticipation of seeing him, and she tried to calm her nerves as she reminded herself to slow down. This was a business opportunity and nothing more.

But when she arrived at the intersection across from the freshly painted sign that read Evan Covington, Attorney at Law, and saw him locking his door as she knew he would at exactly 12:03 p.m., she lost courage. Just as she had yesterday, and the day before that. She did a quick about-face and nearly ran right into Reverend Hindmon's broad girth.

"Oh, I'm so sorry, Reverend. I wasn't watching where I was going."

"That's quite alright, Miss Cooper. It's always a pleasure to see you, even if that pleasure is accompanied by a bruise or two."

Amelia started to respond but was interrupted by a voice behind her.

"Yes, it is always a treat to have Miss Cooper around."

Evan. His voice came from such proximity, she knew he was standing near. She could feel her cheeks turning pink, but there was nothing she could do about that now. With a long, slow breath for poise, she drew herself up to her full height—which only came to the midpoint between Evan's elbow and shoulder—and turned. "Why, Mr. Covington. How nice to see you." Did her voice sound higher than normal?

"The pleasure is all mine." His words soaked into her like warm syrup on a fresh pancake. Reverend Hindmon excused himself and moved on.

Oh, mercy. *Get hold of yourself, Amelia.*

The fact that she had developed the teensiest bit of romantic affection for the man was as much of a shock to her as anything ever had been. Why, it was just over two years ago that she'd lost her dear Gerald. Her intended, a US marshal, had been killed in the line of duty. And she'd vowed she'd never love again.

Yet here she was, mooning over Evan Covington like a besotted schoolgirl, and it came as such a surprise to her, she didn't quite know how to handle it. She knew nothing would come of it. But she supposed it was good in a way. It showed she was ready to step out of her grief. It showed—

"—lunch?" Evan looked at her expectantly.

Oh, dear. He'd been speaking to her, and she had no idea what he'd said. What a dolt she was. "I...I, uhm, apologize, Mr. Covington. My mind was distracted for a moment. Could you repeat the question?"

He smiled at her, a smile that turned her senseless. "I was wondering if I might have the pleasure of your company over lunch, at Market Square. I have a business proposition for you."

A business proposition? Oh. While part of her wanted to shout *Yes!*, she reminded herself not to appear too eager. After all, she was twenty-three years old. She had a promising career as a journalist. She was not some lovesick, husband-hungry hothouse flower who couldn't survive without a man.

Okay. Maybe she was a little lovesick, but she wasn't proud of it. And she certainly didn't have to play the part. "How kind of you, Mr. Covington. I actually have a short amount of time available, though I do have an appointment scheduled for after lunch. I believe I can work you in right now."

~

*F*or a week now, Evan had fought the urge to ask Miss Cooper to lunch. The coming months would be crucial if he was going to establish a solid footing as Houston's up-and-coming lawyer. There was only one other law practice in town, yet the growing community could certainly support three or four lawyers. It wouldn't be long before word got around, and there would be a dozen or more young whippersnappers—much like himself—trying to mark their domain by setting up their own practices.

By that time, Evan needed to already have a good name and reputation. Yes, he'd arrived on the scene at the perfect time, but he needed to make the most of the opportunity. And that certainly didn't involve a five-foot-two blonde, blue-eyed reporter. At least not for a while.

Yet he couldn't keep his mind from wandering to her multiple times a day. And for the past week, he'd caught a glimpse of her each day as he left the office for a quick lunch. Every time, she'd hurried away as if she had some pressing appointment. But today, he'd acted on impulse, darting across the busy street and catching her just as she collided with the reverend. Poor thing must be as busy as he was. Perhaps the newspaper needed to hire another reporter.

Before he thought better of it, he'd blurted out the lunch invitation. A business proposition? Where in the world did that come from? What in the name of good sense had come over him, to say such a thing? Now he'd have to figure out a legitimate business proposal to present to her.

Together they made their way up the four blocks to the restaurant. The streets were too crowded for much conversation, which was a relief. It gave him time to figure out this business venture he supposedly had in mind.

By the time they arrived at Market Square, however, he was still at a loss. He held open the door for her and signaled the waiter for a table for two. Together they followed the man to a place in the back corner of the restaurant. Why, it looked almost planned, like he'd arranged this as a romantic rendezvous. Never mind that it was the only table for two available in the crowded restaurant.

"Thank you, Mr. Covington," she said as he held out her

chair. He seated himself across from her, and his mind still churned in a mental tornado, trying to figure out what he could possibly tell her about this so-called business proposal.

The two sat there in awkward silence for several moments, each studying the menu, until finally he asked, "Do you eat here often?"

"Occasionally. Mostly I eat at my boarding house. Mrs. Green, the proprietress, is a wonderful cook."

"Oh, that's nice."

Another uneasy pause. Talking—eloquently, as a matter of fact—was what Evan did for a living. So why on earth did his tongue feel like it was clothes-pinned to the roof of his mouth?

Amelia—Miss Cooper—placed her menu aside and looked him square on. "So. You want me to interview you."

"Interview?"

"Yes. Isn't that what you wanted to ask me about? An interview, so you can inform the community of your new practice?"

An interview. Of course. "I...hope it's not presumptuous of me to ask. I just thought..."

"Not presumptuous at all, Mr. Covington. We both have a job to do. Yours is to promote your business, and mine is to write stories that sell newspapers. I'll be glad to interview you, though I must say it will be another week or so before I can run the story. With all the new businesses in town, newspaper space is limited. Of course, if you'd like to purchase an advertisement..."

"An advertisement. Yes." Evan didn't know why he hadn't thought of that before. This false business proposal of his was truly turning out to his advantage. Plus, he was having lunch with one of the most attractive women he'd ever met. Altogether, not a bad way to spend his lunch hour.

wo days later, Amelia sat inside Evan's office for the first time, pencil in hand. It was a lovely place of business, she had to admit. Dark wood floors matched the wood molding on the walls and were offset by navy-and-burgundy-striped wallpaper. An ornately carved desk with pedestal legs sat atop a richly woven rug, and the fringed tapestry curtains displayed the same tones as the wallpaper. "You've certainly taken great care in creating a comfortable, inviting place for your clients."

Evan rewarded her with a smile that somehow showed pride and humility at the same time. "Most of this was my father's. I had it sent from Boston. It means the world to me that I get to use it all now in my own office."

Amelia scrawled some notes. This was great stuff for the article. "Tell me about your father."

"He was an exceptional lawyer. But even more than that, he was an honorable man. I miss him very much." Evan stood from the nailhead-trimmed leather chair and walked to a tastefully framed portrait on the wall behind his desk. "This is him when he was about my age. I hope I can become half the man he was."

His voice sounded husky, and Amelia felt a lump forming in her own throat. "I'm sure he'd be very proud of you."

"I hope so."

The bell on the outer office door jangled then, followed by a woman's voice. "Sorry I'm late. Rett spilled honey on his shirt and had to change at the last minute. And of course, I was behind on the ironing—I'd planned to get to that tonight—oh, hello, Amelia." The look of surprise on Elizabeth Smith's face was priceless. Amelia knew Evan's sister had agreed to work as his assistant for a while, but she'd forgotten. And apparently Evan had forgotten to tell his sister about the interview.

"Amelia has agreed to write a story about the business for the paper. I thought it would be good advertising."

Elizabeth lowered herself into the chair next to Amelia. "What a wonderful idea. And I agree, it will be good for business, though I'm not sure you can handle much more business. Your first appointment was to arrive ten minutes ago, and you're booked the entire day."

"Miss Cooper was my first appointment."

Elizabeth looked from her brother to Amelia, then laughed. "Oh. Well in that case, proceed. I'll just mind my own business at my own desk out front."

"I hope you're not too busy to answer a few questions yourself when I'm finished with your brother," Amelia said. A wide smile reached across Elizabeth's face. "Really? You want to interview me?"

"Of course. I want to hear all angles—how you both ended up in Texas, what caused you to stay…"

"You know why I stayed." Elizabeth held up her hand and flashed the simple wedding band she sported there. "As for Evan, I'm not sure why he's still here. If I'd been nearly dragged to the gallows, I think I'd have stirred quite the cloud of dust on my way out."

"You know I could never leave you alone down here," Evan told her, and Amelia admired the easy way the siblings had with one another. "I have to make sure that Ranger treats you right."

Elizabeth's smile spread even wider then, but she said nothing more as she exited the room. Clearly the Ranger was treating her just fine.

~

*E*van smiled as he heard Elizabeth jabber on about the decor, telling the story of each knickknack and bauble. From the way Amelia kept asking questions, she must be getting a lot of material for her story. He wondered if this would turn into a ladies' piece on interior design instead of the business piece he'd hoped for.

Oh, well. It didn't matter much. He had more business than he could handle right now. He glanced at his watch. He had exactly seven minutes and thirty-two, thirty-one seconds to prepare for his next appointment. At least it was for a standard will—not much preparation involved.

The outer bell jangled again, and he heard a man's voice. Soon Elizabeth was at his door. "Ranger Cody Steves is out front. He says you may want to head to the jail. Apparently there's been an arrest, and the man is requesting a lawyer." "Tell him I'll be right there." He handed Elizabeth the stack of papers he'd prepared for his next clients. "When Mr. and Mrs. LeGare arrive, please have them fill these out, and give my apologies."

He was nearly to the door when Amelia touched his arm. "Do you mind if I come along? I think it will add a nice twist to the story."

Hmm...yes, it might, but Evan wasn't too sure that was a good idea. "You're welcome to come, but please keep in mind that anything I discuss with a potential client is confidential. I won't be able to include you in those conversations."

"I understand."

Amelia's eyes took on the bright, piercing expression he'd seen once before, when she was interviewing him while he was in jail. It reminded him a bit of a barracuda, and for some reason, he found it immensely attractive.

CHAPTER 2

*T*here was no getting around the crowd that had gathered in front of the jail. Amelia lost Evan in the scuffle, but she didn't try too terribly hard to keep up. She knew they'd never let her in the jail, anyway. It was good, however, to see the handsome young lawyer in his element. If only she could be a fly on the cell wall as Evan interviewed his potential client.

"He's guilty, I tell you. It's no accident every boat in the harbor has been sabotaged except his." The man next to Amelia added his voice to the hullabaloo.

"Excuse me, sir," Amelia said to get the man's attention. "I'm a reporter with *The Houston Daily*. Can you tell me what's going on?"

"You better believe I'll tell you. That man in there, his name's Giovanni. Franco Giovanni. His fishin' boat has been bringin' in loads of fish, while every other boat in the harbor has been mysteriously gettin' holes in the hull, or runnin' out of coal, or breakin' their nets... Early this morning, Giovanni was seen near Ben Meyer's rig just before Ben discovered his rope had been cut and he'd floated out from the dock. Took four of us to haul him in. All this while Giovanni's boys were unloadin' all the fish again."

Amelia had to admit, the man sounded guilty. "What is your name?"

"O'Riley. Henry O'Riley," the man told her. "And you have a boat, as well?"

"Yes."

"Has your boat been tampered with?"

"Not yet, but mine was sure to be next. I should be out on the water now, earning money for my family, but instead I'm here, makin' sure Giovanni doesn't interfere with anyone else's business, the low-down, rotten, dirty scoundrel. It's just not right to keep honest men from feedin' their young 'uns."

Amelia's pencil could hardly keep up. Boy, was this gonna be a story. Talk about being at the right place at the right time. Amelia thanked the man, got a few statements from others in the crowd, then headed to her office—just a desk in the corner really—to tell Mr. Thomas about what was sure to make the front page. She'd have to finish Evan's interview later. Come to think of it, she had enough to finish his story, too. What an angle. Slick new city lawyer defends boat saboteur.

Of course, she didn't know yet if Evan would actually take the case. Surely not. Surely he wouldn't defend someone who was guilty of such a heartless crime.

~

*E*van watched the man's face closely and tried to make out the thickly accented words.

"Me and my boys, we just-a mindin' our own...how you say...business. We get up early, before anyone else...we work hard, we do good. We...we have success because of much work. We not cheat any man."

If Franco Giovanni was guilty of what he was being accused

of, he was a very good liar. But Evan's gut told him he was innocent. The man seemed simple and straightforward. His words
weren't calculated. He looked Evan in the eye when he spoke,
and he wore an expression of confusion and fear more than
anger.

Yes, he needed to help this man. This was just the kind of job
his father would have encouraged him to take—defending those
who couldn't defend themselves. With Mr. Giovanni's broken
English, and the local prejudice against immigrants taking jobs
from those who were born in the United States, this man had
little chance of ever being set free.

From what Evan could tell, Giovanni had been wrongly
accused. And Evan knew a thing or two about what that felt
like.

"I'll be happy to represent you, Mr. Giovanni. Try to relax.
I'll ask the sheriff to get you something to eat. It may take me
some time to gather all the information I need, but I promise,
I'll do my best to get you out of here."

The man looked like he might cry. *"Molte grazie. Mille grazie."*

Evan didn't know much Italian, but he knew enough to
understand the man was thanking him profusely. "You're
welcome. I'll do what I can." He left Giovanni in his cell, asked
Sheriff Goodman to feed the man breakfast, and took a deep
breath before exiting into the mob that waited out front.
Somehow he had to get to the bottom of this. But no one in this
crowd seemed inclined to an open mind or a fair trial.

He needed to go to the dock. He needed…Giovanni's sons.
He had to find them. But first, he'd have to get away from this
horde of angry fishermen. As politely as he could, he pardoned
and excused and even pushed his way through the throng until
he'd finally broken free. That's when he remembered Amelia.
Where was she?

He didn't see her anywhere. Oh, well. The *Houston Daily*
office was right on the way to the docks. He could stop in for a

moment and offer his apologies for having to cut their interview short. Yes, that's what he'd do. Hopefully she'd be there.

Minutes later, he saw her blonde head through the window. She was bent over the typewriter, pecking away at the keys. Something about that woman just made him smile all over. Which was highly distracting, and hardly what he needed at this stage in his career. Still, good manners dictated that he should offer regrets for the interruption in their appointment. Yes, he was just showing proper deportment. That was all.

She didn't even look up when he opened the door, she was that absorbed in her story. He hoped it was his interview. "Good morning again, Miss Cooper."

"Oh, hello again, Mr. Covington. That was quite the crowd, down at the jail."

"Yes, it was. I'm sorry about all that—"

"Oh, don't be sorry. This is the biggest story since...well, since *your* story, of course. A James Weston Hardy look-alike is hard to compete with. But this..." She indicated the page in her typewriter. "...this is a good story."

"I take it you're not writing up my interview..."

A flush of pink crept into her cheeks, and Evan fought the urge to smile. This woman was strong and intelligent and feisty and...and absolutely adorable.

"No...I'm sorry. I'll get to that as soon as I can, I promise. It was a delightful interview and will make an excellent profile piece. But we can't ignore front-page news."

"Front-page news, eh?" A cold wave of dawning crept through Evan like an arctic wind, and suddenly she wasn't quite so adorable. "And just what, exactly, are you planning to write on that front page of yours?"

"Why, I'm going to report the news." She scrolled up her paper and pulled it out of the typewriter. Looking quite pleased with herself, she read him her opening sentence. "'A series of unfortunate accidents along the Buffalo Bayou have been traced to Mr. Franco Giovanni, an immigrant fisherman whose business has increased while others have suffered losses.'"

Evan fought back several less-than-polite comments. He didn't want to burn any bridges with the press. "Uh...Miss Cooper...if I were you, I'd be careful about implicating a man without a trial."

She looked offended. "I'm not implicating anyone. I'm simply reporting the facts as they've been reported to me."

"Have you spoken to Mr. Giovanni personally?"

"Of course not. You know I haven't. But I've spoken to several of the men whose boats have been tampered with, and all the evidence points back to Giovanni."

"Miss Cooper, I strongly urge you to wait before you print that...that...drivel."

She sucked in a sharp breath and stood up. "Drivel? How dare you call my work drivel?"

Great. Now he'd done it. Why couldn't he have just kept his mouth shut? Oh, yeah. Because Mr. Giovanni was his client, and it was his job to protect him from being convicted before his case ever went to trial.

"You're right, Miss Cooper. Perhaps drivel was too strong a word. But certainly you understand the importance of—"

"I understand quite well, Mr. Covington. Clearly you've agreed to represent a man who would deprive other hard-working men of their livelihood, simply so he can get ahead in his business. Well, you have your job to do, and I have mine. So if you'll please excuse me, I have an article to finish."

And just like that, she reinserted her paper and began typing again, shutting him out as plainly as if she'd slammed the door in his face. Though there was no door between them at the moment, there was an obvious emotional wall made of several layers of brick and cement. And it looked like it would take a pretty powerful sledgehammer to break it down.

~

*T*he nerve of that man. Amelia typed so fast her fingers nearly lost control, and she knew she'd have to retype the entire report. She'd already made several big errors and was bound to make more before she finished. But her jaw was set, her shoulders clenched, and she didn't dare look up from her task until she knew good and well Mr. Evan Covington had exited the building.

Even after she heard the bell jingle, signaling that he was gone, she kept typing for good measure. Just in case he watched through the window. Then, after enough time had passed, she tore the sheet from the machine and spun in her chair under pretense of reading the contents. But really, she just wanted to make sure a tall lawyer wasn't watching her.

He wasn't, and she felt relief and disappointment at the same time. Was he really going to represent Mr. Giovanni, after what he'd done?

Technically, Evan was right and she knew it. She should try to get both sides of the story before putting something in print that was hard to take back. Mr. Thomas wouldn't be happy if he had to issue a retraction. Still, she'd spoken to four different people, and the stories were all the same. While the other boats had recently been vandalized, Giovanni's boat had been left alone. And he'd hauled in more fish than anybody in the area.

Smelled awful fishy to her.

Normally she would have laughed at her own pun, but today she was too angry. She didn't know if she was more upset at having her journalistic integrity questioned, or at the thought of Evan defending a guilty client. Both were equally disturbing.

And most disturbing of all was the idea that she'd felt an attraction to a man who would defend a guilty party, all in the name of the almighty dollar. She'd thought him above that. Well, it wasn't the first time she'd been wrong, and it probably wouldn't be the last.

Still, it was a concept she found tough to swallow.

The bell jangled again, and this time it was Mr. Thomas. "Time to set the presses. Whatcha got for me?"

Amelia handed him the paper. "I have to retype it."

The man scanned the story and handed it back to her. "Too one-sided. Go interview Giovanni or one of the sons." Then he walked to his office at the back of the building without another word.

She wanted to wad up the paper and throw it at her boss, but she refrained. Instead, she grabbed a fresh notepad and a couple of sharpened pencils and headed back out the door, toward the jail. But she couldn't get within a block of the place, and she wasn't really in the mood to try. Hmm... Maybe the docks. Maybe one of the sons was down there with the boat. Or was there a wife? A sister? A friend? Surely at the docks she'd find someone close to the Giovanni family who'd be willing to speak on their behalf.

~

"*A*nything you can tell me about your whereabouts early this morning will be helpful." Evan questioned Antonio, the older Giovanni son, but was having a hard time with the language barrier. "I tell you one-uh, two-uh, tree times already. We leave in the middle of night. Is how we do in old country. Fish jump into nets in middle of night. That is why we have more fish than those who wait until morning."

"So you were fishing early this morning?"

"We were coming in just as the others were going out."

"Your father was spotted near Mr. Meyer's boat about the time his rope was cut. Can you explain that?"

Antonio took Evan by the arm and led him down the dock.

15

He stopped in front of a small store that sold fishing supplies. "We needed new net. Our old one got caught, got hole in it. Papa came here to order it." Then Antonio turned to the pier directly in front of the store. "That is where Meester Meyer docks his boat."

It made more sense now. The evidence against Franco Giovanni was circumstantial. Evan needed to go straightaway and speak to Sheriff Goodman. If they had nothing more than hearsay, surely they wouldn't hold the man. Then again, Evan had nearly hanged because he looked too much like a fuzzy picture on a flyer. He was still learning that Texas law wasn't exactly the same as law enforcement in other parts of the country.

He was just saying goodbye to Antonio when Miss Cooper approached. Her demeanor toward him was cool, but at least she'd followed his advice to hear all sides of the story. He hoped that was why she was there, anyway.

Evan tipped his hat to her and continued on his way, but he thought he felt her glare burning into his shoulders for several yards. As a lawyer, he knew he might make some enemies along the way. It came with the territory. But making an enemy of Miss Amelia Cooper made him feel sick all the way to his bones.

"$\mathcal{H}$ere." Amelia laid the copy on Mr. Thomas's desk and walked away.

"What's this?"

"Your story. It's no longer one-sided." She heard the man pick up the paper and knew he scanned it for content.

"Better. We'll run it in tomorrow's paper. Hey, come back."

Amelia stopped, wheeled around and walked back to her boss's desk. "Yes?"

He peered at her over the top of his glasses, as if trying to figure out the source of her sour mood, but didn't question her about it. "You have that story on Covington?"

Really? Evan Covington was the last person she wanted to think about. "Not yet. I've done the interview. I just have to compile my notes into a story. I didn't think you'd need it until next week."

"He's high-profile. People still see him as something of a novelty. Unless a big story breaks between now and Friday, I don't have much to fill the weekend edition. I'll run your interview then. Gotta sell papers."

"I'm on it, boss." Amelia turned again, but Mr. Thomas called her back.

"Not so fast. I also want you to start checking in daily with the Rangers. See if there's anything to report. People are fascinated with them, as well."

"They're not going to tell me anything."

"They will if you play nice. Bake a pie or something. They may not give you the hard stuff, but they might throw us a bone or two. I thought we'd start a new column, call it the 'Ranger Report.' I'll head over there when I leave in a while, talk with that head guy. Ray, isn't it?"

Amelia nodded. "Captain Ray McCoy."

"Yeah, that's the guy. I'll let him know you'll be stopping in. But be nice, okay? See if you can get the lowdown."

"You really want me to bake a pie?"

"Not unless you want to. But if you do, bring me a slice." Mr. Thomas went back to his typesetting, and she knew she was dismissed.

～

*T*he next day, Evan held his copy of *The Houston Daily* and shook his head. There it was. Front page. To her credit, Miss Cooper had included quotes from Giovanni's family, claiming his innocence. But the article was still heavily slanted, in Evan's opinion.

Goodman refused to release the man. Said it was for his own safety, and now Evan was inclined to agree. Why, it looked like he'd already been tried and convicted. If he went free now, there was a good chance people would take justice—their perceived justice, anyway—into their own hands.

He wasn't sure how to proceed from here. Wished his father were around. He'd know what to do. Evan paced back and forth in his office until Elizabeth appeared in the doorway.

"Pacing won't help, you know."

"I know. But I can't sit still. I can't believe that woman would—"

"She's just doing her job. You know that."

"But her job is causing an innocent man harm."

"I've seen you read that paper every day since your release. Have you ever had a problem with her reporting before?"

"Not that I recall."

"Well, this is the first time her story has affected one of your clients. Let me see." Elizabeth took the paper from his hands and sat in one of the tufted leather chairs reserved for clients. "She represented both sides."

"But not equally."

"Aren't there more people in this town who consider Giovanni guilty than innocent?"

"Everyone but his family thinks he's guilty."

"Then I'd say she accurately represented what the general population feels."

"But it's not true."

"It's her job to report what she heard and not misrepresent people's quotes. It's your job to prove him innocent. You can't hold it against her for doing her job any more than she can hold it against you for doing yours."

Maybe Elizabeth was right. But Evan still didn't like it.

"I think you're sweet on her," Elizabeth said.

"What?"

"I see the way you look at her."

"I don't know what you're—"

Elizabeth held up her hand to stop him. "Don't forget, you're talking to the one person in this world who's known you the longest, and who knows you best."

Evan snatched the newspaper from his sister and returned to his own chair, behind his desk. "I'll admit, Miss Cooper is an attractive woman."

"And...?"

"And what? There is nothing more." "And you would like to know her better."

Evan held up the newspaper. "I know plenty. Thank you very much. Your services as meddler and all-around busybody are no longer required here."

Elizabeth opened her mouth and closed it once or twice, then promptly stood and left the room. A moment later she leaned her head back through his doorway. "Would you like to join us for dinner tomorrow evening? Say, around seven o'clock?"

"Yes, sister. That sounds lovely. Thank you for the invitation."

$\sim$

"*M*iss Cooper. We've been expecting you." Lieutenant Rett Smith motioned to a wooden chair in front of his desk. "Your boss, Mr. Thomas, stopped by yesterday. He said you'd have pie..."

Amelia laughed. She could see why Rett's sister, Elizabeth, had been so taken with the man. He had an easy charm about him that most women would be drawn to. Not her, though. She was done with men wearing badges. "Ranger Smith, trust me. I could make you a cake or a pie or whatever you want. But you probably wouldn't like it much. I'm far better at writing about recipes than actually following them."

Rett laughed. "Well, at least you know your strengths. That's always a good thing." He reached toward a stack of papers on the corner of his desk. "I've prepared a list of misdemeanors that we've dealt with in the last week. I've not included names, and of course we can't reveal details about more serious crimes until they've been fully investigated, tried and convicted. Or acquitted, whichever the case."

Amelia took the paper. "I understand. And thank you. This should provide enough to hold our readers' curiosity, at least for a while."

As she spoke, she heard the door open and close behind her and watched Rett's face light up.

"Hey, pretty lady," Rett said to the person behind her, and Amelia knew it was Elizabeth. She turned to greet her friend as well.

"Hello, stranger. I'm a little put out with your husband, because he doesn't share you with me as much as I'd like," Amelia teased.

"Between my husband and my brother, I hardly have time to turn around," Elizabeth admitted. "And I don't have much time now." She looked at Rett. "I was hoping you could stop at the bakery and get a pie on your way home?"

"Sure. What kind?"

"Your choice." Then she looked at Amelia. "Why don't you come over for dinner tonight? Seven o'clock. Please say yes. I won't take no for an answer."

"Seven? I think that will work. What can I bring?"

"Not a thing. Just yourself."

"Why don't you let me make the pie? I have to pass right by the bakery, anyway."

Rett laughed at her attempt at humor, and Elizabeth just nodded. "If you wish. It's all settled, then. I have to get back. I'll see you at seven." Elizabeth smiled at Amelia like she knew a secret, but Amelia brushed it off while the newlyweds shared a quick hug.

It made her happy and sad at the same time to see her friends so much in love. Deep down, she wanted that for herself. She'd had it once, with Gerald, and for that she was grateful. At least she'd known that kind of affection. Some people never found it. Evan's face appeared in her thoughts, and she worked to push the image away. No. Evan Covington might be a handsome man, but he was not the man for her. She could never be interested in a man who would represent a crook like Giovanni.

Several hours later, she had typed up the "Ranger Report," put the finishing touches on Evan's—Mr. Covington's—interview, and picked up an apple pie and two dozen ladyfingers. She'd even had time to swing by the boarding house, freshen up a bit and let Mrs. Green know she wouldn't be taking dinner. She was just rounding the corner to Rett and Elizabeth's home when she nearly bumped into, of all people, Evan Covington.

"Good day, Miss Cooper," he said, and his voice sounded tight.

"Good evening, Mr. Covington," she replied, then lifted her chin and kept walking. Unfortunately, he was walking the same direction. All the way up the street they walked in stiff silence, until they reached the Smith home and it became clear they'd both arrived at their destination.

"I've been invited to share dinner with my sister," Evan confessed.

Rats. "So have I."

They stood there in balky silence for a moment. Finally Evan reached out. "May I carry your packages for you, then?"

"That's very kind of you, but no. I've got them."

Evan gestured for her to go ahead of him on the sidewalk.

The door opened just as they reached the front steps. "Perfect. I'm so glad you came together. The roast is just about ready." Elizabeth held the door for them. "Here, Amelia, let me take those. Oh, they look delicious. Apple is Rett's favorite. Mine too, but it's tied with chocolate. And ladyfingers. You didn't have to…"

"I try not to keep sweets in my room, so whatever doesn't get eaten stays here," Amelia told her, grateful for the chance to focus on something besides the good-looking annoyance standing behind her. It was going to be a long evening.

~

*E*van tried to concentrate on his sister's delicious cooking and not on the stunning, exasperating woman seated to his right. Why, those sweet eyes might have fooled him for a time, but not anymore. No, sir. That face hid the heart of an urchin.

"Evan, how is the Giovanni case coming? I didn't get a chance to ask you about it this afternoon." Elizabeth smiled her trying-to-look-innocent smile, and Evan wanted to strangle her. Might have if Rett hadn't been sitting there, still wearing his Ranger badge.

"Yes, Mr. Covington. How is that coming for you?" Amelia's tone was neutral, but Evan knew. She was baiting him.

"It's coming quite well, thank you, despite efforts of our local press to convict the man without a trial."

Amelia placed her fork down a little too forcefully, and it clanked on her plate. "The press has done nothing of the sort, Mr. Covington. It's the press's job to report the news as it happens. Mr. Giovanni's case is news right now."

"I wouldn't have a problem with *The Houston Daily* reporting the story if their reporters would get their facts straight before printing them."

"And just what facts did *The Houston Daily* misrepresent, Mr. Covington?"

"You—I mean *the paper*—filled your readers' minds with images of Mr. Giovanni as guilty."

"How? How did we misconstrue the images, as you say?"

"Time and again in the article, Giovanni was referred to as 'the accused.' You listed all of these horrendous things and attached his name to them as if he were guilty."

"Mr. Giovanni was referred to as 'the accused' because that's what he is. He's been accused of something. The article didn't imply he was either guilty or innocent, simply that he's been accused."

"In so doing, the article made him look guilty, and you know it." Evan worked to keep his voice calm, but it was hard.

Finally, Elizabeth pushed her chair back and began gathering their plates, even though Evan hadn't finished. "I believe it's time for some apple pie and ladyfingers. Rett, would you help me in the kitchen, please?"

The kitchen was really an extension of the dining and sitting room, but Elizabeth and Rett retreated to the far corner of the room nonetheless.

Amelia wiped her mouth daintily with her napkin and replaced it in her lap. "Mr. Covington." She cleared her throat as if weighing her next words carefully. "I do apologize if my doing my job has in any way made your job more difficult. But I believe in our justice system, and as a lawyer, I hope you believe in it as well. If the man is innocent, it will all come out in court."

"Of course I believe in our justice system, Miss Cooper. But it's not without its flaws, and we both know it. Giovanni will most likely be tried by a jury. If that jury has already been convinced of his guilt because of something they've read in the paper, he won't have a fair chance."

The back door opened and shut, and Evan realized his sister and brother-in-law had stepped outside. Probably under the pretense of feeding the scraps to the half-dozen chickens in their backyard. Evan knew better. The stillness stretched into taciturnity, as neither seemed to have anything else to add to the conversation. Finally Amelia took a deep breath and heaved a great sigh. "If only there were someone else. Someone with motive to keep the other fishermen from succeeding at their business. Have you considered the possibility that Giovanni has been framed?"

Evan leaned forward. "Yes. But everyone I've spoken to has

had their boat tampered with in some way. Everyone but Giovanni."

Amelia's eyebrows lifted, wrinkling her smooth forehead. "Not everyone."

~

ell, the evening wasn't a total failure, after all. Following an extremely uncomfortable exchange during dinner, Amelia had been ready to excuse herself early. But then she and Evan had actually connected on the possibility that perhaps they could both do their jobs, and do them well, without hindering each other. Why, they'd even figured out a way to help one another, and Amelia felt exhilarated that such an intelligent, educated man as Evan Covington actually seemed interested, even hungry, for her thoughts.

By the time the stars were out and the foursome had partaken of more than their share of dessert, coffee and laughter, Evan and Amelia were on pleasant terms once again. At least they could be friends, though Amelia had put the lawyer out of her mind as a romantic interest. No.

It would never work.

At the door, Evan held out his elbow. "Might I have the pleasure of accompanying you back to your boarding house, Miss Cooper?"

"I'd be honored, Mr. Covington," she replied, trying to ignore the glint in Elizabeth Smith's eyes. That the woman was playing matchmaker was obvious. It was a compliment, to say the least, to be considered a worthy match for her brother. But the last few days had proven to Amelia that her own ambitions were at odds with Mr. Covington's. Friends, yes. They could be friends. Nothing more.

Still, with the moon casting its soft glow on their path and a million stars cheering them on, Amelia couldn't help but pretend a little bit. It would be nice to have a real beau again someday.

"What has you so deep in thought?" Evan asked.

"Oh...just remembering."

"Remembering what, if I might be so bold?"

Amelia stopped in the road. "Gerald—my fiancé—and I used to go on moonlight walks."

Evan's face changed, and he took a step back. "Your fiancé? I'm sorry. I didn't realize—"

"No. He's not my fiancé any more. He...he was a US deputy marshal, and he was killed in the line of duty. That was just over two years ago."

Evan stepped forward again, this time placing his hand in the small of her back. "I'm sorry. I didn't know."

"It's getting easier. Time heals all wounds, they say. At least I know never to get involved with a man who shoots bad guys for a living."

"Elizabeth has the same fears for Rett. So far, he's stayed close to home. But one of these days, he'll be called away for a time, and I'm afraid Elizabeth will be sick with worry until he returns."

"The last time he had to leave on assignment, she went with him." Amelia smiled at the recollection, and so did Evan. The last time Rett's duties as a Ranger had required he travel away from home, it was to find the real James Weston Hardy. It was when Elizabeth and Rett had fallen in love. And that journey ultimately saved Evan from being hanged.

"I sometimes wonder if we'll hear from the Hardy gang again," Evan started a slow walk but didn't remove his hand from her back. "Other than the one fellow who was shot, they got away."

The warmth of his touch stirred something wonderful and awful in Amelia's spirit. It wasn't so much that she missed

Gerald. It was more that she didn't remember ever feeling this affected by Gerald.

"Surely they know better than to return to Houston. Ideally they'll be caught soon. At least they're someone else's problem for the time being."

Evan nodded. They were at the boarding house now. Amelia thanked him for escorting her and bid him good night. But it was a very long time before she fell asleep.

CHAPTER 4

"*H*ello, Mr. O'Riley. My name is Evan Covington. Might I have a moment of your time?"

The man sat with his feet dangling over the edge of the dock. He was mending some kind of rope. "Ain't you Giovanni's lawyer?"

"Yes, sir, I am."

"Then no. I ain't got time for the likes of you."

"I understand yours is the only boat out here, other than Giovanni's, that hasn't been tampered with."

"So?"

"Why do you think that is, Mr. O'Riley?"

"Because I keep a close eye on things, that's why. Go away. I'm busy."

"So you're saying you keep a closer watch on things than any other man out here, besides Giovanni and his sons?"

"Mebbe so. Why are you still here?" The man spat into the water and continued braiding three strands of the rope together.

"Just trying to get my facts straight. I understand you were the one who first reported Giovanni to the authorities." O'Riley laid the rope down then, stood and approached Evan until their faces were just inches apart. The man stood eye to eye with Evan, but his girth was considerably larger than Evan's slim frame. The threat in his stance was unmistakable. "Just exactly what are you getting at?"

"As I said, I'm just keeping my facts straight."

"Well, while you're straightening out those facts, you might want to keep those pretty white teeth straight as well. I said, go away."

Evan held his ground. Didn't say a word, but didn't back away either. The two men stood there for an uncomfortable amount of time, and O'Riley's breath made Evan's stomach roil. Still, he refused to be bullied by a barking dog. And considering O'Riley had been the dog who'd barked the loudest about Mr. Giovanni, Evan had some pretty strong suspicions about who was actually responsible for the crimes at the dock.

"Is there a problem here, gentlemen?" Ranger Captain Ray McCoy approached them, and O'Riley backed away.

"No sir. No problem at all," the fisherman said to Ray, though his eyes remained on Evan. "Pretty boy here was just leaving."

Evan held O'Riley's eyes until the man reseated himself and continued work on his rope.

"Mr. Covington, might I have a word with you?" Ray asked, and the two started down the dock away from the man.

"What can I do for you, Ranger?"

Ray laughed. "That was some show of bravado back there. That guy is twice your size. Mean, too."

"I refuse to be intimidated by the likes of Henry O'Riley. Or any man, for that matter. Bullying shows a lack of morals and an overriding sense of cowardice."

"That may be true, but for a minute there I thought I was gonna have to carry you back to your sister. And we both know she wouldn't have been happy about that. Why, we'd have had to pull her off of him if he'd have messed up those pretty teeth."

"How long were you standing there?"

"Long enough. I must admit, I'm impressed. You've got the stuff Rangers are made of."

Evan laughed. "No thanks. I already have a job. Were you looking for me?"

"No. Just patrolling the docks. If I were you, I'd always take a witness along if you need to speak to O'Riley. He's got a mouth on him, as you heard. And though he's never gotten into any real trouble, there's something about him I don't trust."

"That makes two of us," Evan said before he tipped his hat to the Ranger and headed back to his office.

But when he opened the door, there was Amelia, sitting in one of the chairs in the waiting area. "Oh, hello, Miss Cooper. This is a nice surprise. Were you waiting for me?"

She blushed then, and Evan tried to hold back his goofy smile that always showed up whenever she was around.

"No...I, uh—"

"Don't be so vain, Evan," Elizabeth said. "She's waiting for me. We're sharing lunch together, but I didn't want to lock up until you got back. Would you like to join us? I could see if Rett's free, and we could make it a foursome." Elizabeth had that cat-ate-the-canary grin, and he knew she was playing match-maker again. When would she get it through her head? Evan didn't have time for a romance. And he and Miss Cooper were just friends.

But he had to admit. Life—and lunch—was certainly more pleasant when Miss Amelia Cooper was involved.

*O*ver the next few weeks, Amelia's life fell into an unexpected routine. She was still in charge of the society page. She still interviewed local women and printed their favorite recipes or wrote about new dress patterns. Though she poured her heart into making these articles interesting, it was difficult writing about things in which she had no interest.

At least Mr. Thomas had loosened the reins a bit and let her write the "Ranger Report." Still, that was more a list than an actual article. No room for creativity. Her only hope for writing about real news was if she just happened to be at the right place at the right time and got the scoop before anyone else.

Like the story of boat tampering at the docks. Or Evan's story of mistaken identity, for that matter. In those two cases, Mr. Thomas actually printed her articles. But he never assigned stories to her. He'd write them himself or hire an outsider to write them, which annoyed her to no end. But she was grateful for her job and tried not to complain too much. If only Mr. Thomas believed in her like… Like Evan.

Despite their initial disagreement over the Giovanni story, Evan had become a supportive and encouraging friend. Why, he read all of her society page columns and told her how well-written they were. Imagine that.

When she did the story on the deaf seamstress who'd moved all the way to Houston from some small town in Kentucky to open a dress shop, he'd let her practice her sign language on him. When she had to sample six different macaroon recipes, he'd eagerly offered his help. And when she reported on the wedding of the year—the mayor's daughter to the preacher's son—he'd read every word and told her that Mr. Thomas was far underestimating her abilities.

Too bad she and Evan would only ever be just friends. But it was best this way, she knew. She wished her brain would tell that to her heart, or her nerves, or whatever it was that caused her pulse to quicken every time he was near.

Like now. The bell on the door jangled. "Good day, Miss Cooper."

He was early. For the last week, he'd stopped in around noon every day to see if she wanted to eat lunch with him. It had become a routine, yet they both acted like it was a random event, as if they just happened to have some free time and were looking for a companion to share it with.

"Why, hello, Mr. Covington. What a pleasant surprise." They shared a smile then. They both knew it was no surprise.

"I was wondering if you might like to share the lunch hour with me, or if you have other plans."

"No other plans. I'd love to join you. I brought an extra ham sandwich today, as well as some of Mrs. Green's turnovers, if you'd like to share."

"If you're sure there's enough."

"Oh, I have more than enough, Mr. Covington." She'd made sure of it. A couple of days they'd had lunch in Market Square. Yesterday they'd purchased a link sausage from the vendor on the corner. But this morning, when Mrs. Green made far too many pastries, she'd asked the woman to tuck them and an extra sandwich into her lunch.

She grabbed her most recent article—about the benefits of cutting a pattern on the bias—and placed the pages in her basket. Evan always wanted to see what she was working on.

He held out his arm for her, and she took hold, as had become their custom. Together they walked toward the newly appointed Central Park. Really, the place was just a wooded lot with a few benches and tables. But the city council had big plans, and she'd surely be writing about those plans one day soon.

Just as they were about to turn onto the street leading to the park, however, Mr. O'Riley approached. "I should have known the likes of the two of you would be cavorting around town together."

"Pardon me?" Evan said.

"Why, you and your lady friend here have set me up. Giovanni's been released from jail. Not enough evidence, they said. Plan to investigate more, they said. And to make matters worse, the authorities are questioning me. Lots of my fellow fishermen, too. Friends I've known for years are lookin' at me with suspicious eyes. And it's all your fault." O'Riley pointed at Amelia.

"My fault? What did I do?" Amelia asked.

"You printed my name in that story of yours, and now it's come back on me. Well, I'm gonna sue you and your paper for damaging my reputation."

"But I—"

Evan interrupted her. "Don't even respond to such nonsense, Miss Cooper."

"What, are you her lawyer too? Let her speak for herself." O'Riley became more agitated the more he spoke.

"Mr. O'Riley, you shared with me freely. You even spelled your name for me when I asked. I wrote nothing in the article that wasn't true. And I don't recall your asking me to keep our conversation confidential. You knew I was from the newspaper, and you talked to me of your own accord. *The Houston Daily* was well within its rights to print what you said."

"You better watch yourself. Both of you."

"Is that a threat, Mr. O'Riley?" Evan asked.

"Take it any way you want to. Just stay out of my business."

Evan placed a firm hand on her back and guided her away from the angry man. When they reached their favorite bench at the park, he motioned for her to sit, but he remained standing. Began pacing, as a matter of fact.

"Did you know Giovanni had been released?" Amelia asked.

"Of course I knew. I was there."

"You could have told me."

"I don't make it a habit of discussing my cases with the press."

Amelia bristled, but she wasn't offended. Of course he wouldn't talk to her about the case. Swirling around, she plopped down on the bench and held the basket in her lap. "Are you worried? Because you look worried." She wasn't sure if she should unpack their lunch or just wait for him to sit.

"I'm not worried about him suing your newspaper. He doesn't have a case. But I am worried about you. I don't trust the man. If I hadn't been with you today, there's no telling what he would have done."

"Do you think he's guilty of damaging the other boats? Do you think he really did try to set Giovanni up?"

"It wouldn't surprise me. But if I were you, I'd let Mr. Thomas write any further news stories involving O'Riley."

Amelia froze. Did he really say what she thought he'd said? "Why? Just because I'm a woman?"

"Yes…no…partly. Partly because you're a woman. Partly because—face it, Amelia. You're very small."

He'd called her Amelia.

"And partly because I'm not sure how much protection Mrs. Green can offer you. You're an unmarried woman, living on your own under the protection of an elderly woman and a few other female boarders."

"There's Mr. Mitchell, the postmaster. He lives there, too."

"He's eighty-four."

This entire conversation only served to remind Amelia that, although Evan's company was a pleasant distraction, they could never, ever be more than friends. He simply didn't understand. She wasn't sure any man ever would.

"Mr. Covington, I am a reporter. I write the news. I will not let some loathsome, fishy-smelling boatmonger scare me from doing my job."

"Fishmonger."

"What?"

"I believe the word is fishmong—never mind. Let's speak of something else, shall we?"

"I think that's an excellent idea." Amelia removed the sandwiches and handed one to Evan, but her motions were stiff and jerky. She'd never been very good at hiding her feelings.

Evan unwrapped his sandwich and examined it. "Do you know where the sandwich got its name?"

"What?"

"John Montagu, the Fourth Earl of Sandwich."

"What in the world are you talking about?"

Evan held up his sandwich. "John Montagu was an English aristocrat. He lived over a hundred years ago and was fond of poker."

Amelia looked at Evan's sandwich, then back at him. "Okay..."

"While playing the game, he requested that his butler bring him a slab of meat between two slices of bread. That way, he could eat with one hand and hold his cards with the other and not get the cards all greasy by eating meat with his bare hands."

"And you're telling me this because..."

"I think it's an interesting story. Soon, the other men at the table began requesting the same from the butler. 'I'll have the same as Sandwich,' they'd say. And voilà. The sandwich was born."

"I doubt that's the first time anyone had meat between two slices of bread."

"Probably not. But it is, however, the way this particular meal got its name."

Amelia smiled then. It was hard to stay mad at Evan. He had a way of making her grin even when she didn't want to. Feeling the tightness in her shoulders relax, she unwrapped her sandwich and took a bite.

CHAPTER 5

"Y ou have to talk some sense into her," Evan told
Elizabeth as soon as he returned to the office that
afternoon. "She won't listen to me."

"You told her not to report on the boat story. I'm not sure I
understand your reasoning. Even if she refrains from writing
this story, there's bound to be another story at some point in the
future in which she'll have to implicate someone in a crime.
You've even said it yourself. She's got a gift and she needs to
use it."

"That was before I realized she might be endangering
herself. Besides, it's hardly appropriate for a young woman to be
gallivanting around, interviewing a bunch of rough fishermen."

"That's her job. And you've never been overly concerned
with propriety before, Evan."

"This isn't about propriety. It's about her safety. If she's
going to do a man's work, she needs some kind of protection.
Maybe she can get a firearm, like one of those women in the
vaudeville shows. Only hers won't be for show…"

"Now you sound like Rett. He's afraid that since all the
members of Hardy's gang weren't captured, they'll come back

for retribution. He's afraid to leave me alone. And... don't tell anyone..." She lowered her voice, even though they were the only ones present. "He got me my very own Deringer."

"Can you hit a target?"

"At close range I can."

Evan looked at his sister, but he didn't have any idea what to say.

Elizabeth set her pencil down and leaned back in her chair. "You could just marry her."

"What? No. That's preposterous."

"Why? You're in love with her."

"I most certainly am not. Miss Cooper is a friend and nothing more. Besides, I'm in no position to consider marriage at the moment. I need to get this business up and running."

"Looks to me like it's up. It's running. You have more work than you need."

"Yes, but it's not established yet. I'm getting business because I'm still a novelty. The amount of business I have in the future will depend on how well I do my job now. If I allow myself to become distracted with courtship and marriage, people will get the idea I'm not a serious lawyer, and they'll take their business elsewhere."

"Or they may view you as more settled, since you have a wife. But courtship or not, Miss Cooper has already become quite a distraction for you."

Evan plopped down in a chair opposite Elizabeth's desk. "Yes, it would seem so. But it's only because I'm grateful. She did help me, after all, when I was imprisoned. She believed in my innocence when few others did."

"Hmm..." Elizabeth shuffled some papers on her desk in obvious pretense of being busy.

"Out with it."

"Out with what?"

"You only say 'hmm' like that when you've got something on your mind. So say it."

"I've already said it, dear brother. You're in love with Amelia Cooper, and the more you deny it, the harder you fall. And I'm almost certain she feels the same way about you."

"Nonsense. She barely spoke to me at lunch today. I doubt she'll even make time for me tomorrow."

"Yet she endures the same attitude from Mr. Thomas. He doesn't like her doing hard news, either. Yet his manner doesn't seem to ruffle her overly much. Why do you think it upset her coming from you?"

"He pays her. I don't."

"All right. Whatever you say. But you know, you could always work with her on the story. Anything the two of you learn to implicate this Mr. O'Riley will only help clear Mr. Giovanni's name." Elizabeth went back to her papers.

Evan excused himself to his office. He'd spent the better part of the morning at the jail, seeing to Giovanni's release, and he was already behind on two wills and a land lease agreement.

~

"Giovanni was released this morning," Mr. Thomas told Amelia when she returned to the office.

"I know. I heard."

"Normally I'd take over the story, but the missus has a bad cough, and I told her I'd try to cut out early and check on her. You okay with carrying it?"

"Do you have to ask?"

"That's what I thought. I've already spoken to the sheriff, but you'll need to do some follow-up down at the docks."

"I'm on it, boss. I hope Mrs. Thomas feels better."

"I'll tell her you said so. And hey—" he waited until Amelia was looking at him. "Be careful, okay? No snooping around after dark. I want you out of there by five o'clock. The place gets pretty deserted after that."

"Aye, aye, cap'n." Amelia saluted, and Mr. Thomas just shook his head, grunted, and left.

Something in Amelia had urged her to tell him about the encounter with O'Riley, but…well…it didn't really come up. And he'd have pulled her from the story. And his wife was sick. He didn't need to worry about Amelia. She felt justified in keeping it from him…sort of. Well, it was too late now.

She grabbed a clean writing tablet from the stack on the shelf and a couple of sharpened pencils and headed out the door. She'd show Mr. Evan Covington. She was perfectly capable of doing her job and taking care of herself. What did being a woman and small have to do with anything anyway?

Quite a few of the boats were missing from their berths, and Amelia knew the fishermen were still out trying to catch fish. Those who fished at night sat around making repairs and comparing their recent catches. A couple of boats had just pulled in, bringing the stench of fish and seaweed with them.

Men whistled as she walked by, but she ignored them. She knew women didn't typically wander around the docks unaccompanied. But it was broad daylight, she was wearing her press badge and she had her tablet and pencils. They had no reason to think she was there for purposes other than journalism.

Still, she looked around for the safest-looking character she could find. One man—she couldn't tell if he was ancient or just wrinkled from the sun—whistled "When I Survey the Wondrous Cross" while he examined a net. Perfect.

"Excuse me, sir?"

The man stopped whistling and smiled, causing the creases in his face to turn into canyons. "What can I do fer ye, miss?" The man's Irish lilt and short stature reminded her of a leprechaun.

"I'm Amelia Cooper with *The Houston Daily*, and I was wondering if I might ask you a few questions?"

"Ask away. I'd much rather spend me time talkin' to a pretty lady than checkin' over these nets."

Amelia smiled. "Thank you. I'm writing a follow-up article about the recent damage that has occurred to some boats and fishing supplies. Have you experienced any of that?"

The man's face fell. "Unfortunately, yes. Several weeks ago, I got out to sea only to find all me nets had been cut through the middle. That's why I check every one when I get in each day and before I go out the next morning. Takes quite a bit more time to check them twice a day instead of once, but I can't take the risk. I lost an entire day's labor—and wages. Not to mention the cost of replacin' the nets. They were irreparable."

"I'm sorry to hear that." Amelia scribbled away in her tablet. The lead on her pencil broke, and she pulled out her spare. "Do you have any idea who might be responsible for these mishaps?"

The man took her broken pencil, pulled out a pocketknife, and began sharpening it. "I have me ideas. But I'm not about to point a finger at any man. I didn't see anything with me own eyes, so I'd rather not comment."

"I understand. Do you mind if I include your comments and your name in my upcoming report?"

"Not at all. I've not said anything to ye that I wouldn't say to anyone who asked. The name's Murphy. Sean Murphy."

"Thank you, Mr. Murphy. I'll let you get back to your work."

The man nodded, handed her the freshly sharpened pencil and whistled once again as he picked up his nets. Now to find someone else who looked safe. She walked several paces up the dock but stopped when she saw O'Riley headed in her direction. And he looked very, very angry.

~

*S*omething had pulled Evan toward the docks. He needed to talk to Giovanni about his case, but he knew the man was home with his wife and sons. He wouldn't show up at his boat for several more hours. Still, a feeling in his gut told Evan he needed to head that way now. Maybe he could question a few more people down there.

When he turned the corner in the path that led to the docks, he knew exactly why he was supposed to go early. About fifty yards ahead of him was O'Riley, towering over Amelia in full swagger, clearly harassing her.

But she didn't look shaken. Instead, she stood in quiet repose and let the man have his say. Several fishermen observed, and one older man walked up behind her, standing several steps back as if to let O'Riley know of his presence.

As Evan drew closer, he could hear bits of the conversation.

"I'll not stand for you snoopin' around here any more, missy."

"Mr. O'Riley, this is a public dock. You can't keep me from being down here."

"I can have you arrested for harassment."

"I assure you, Mr. O'Riley, it's not me who is doing the harassing."

O'Riley looked up then, as if aware for the first time that he had an audience. The fishermen who had watched with interest suddenly turned back to their tasks, except for the older man. When O'Riley's eyes finally landed on Evan, his face turned red and he clenched his fists...but said nothing more. Just turned around and stomped back to his boat.

That's when Amelia, recognizing someone was behind her, turned. She smiled at the older man, but the smile shrank and she looked rather irritated when she saw Evan. Quite a difference from the delighted expression he'd been rewarded with at her office, just before lunch.

41

"Spying on me, Mr. Covington?"

"No, ma'am, Miss Cooper. I have a job to do, same as you."

"I see." She turned her attention back to the older man. "Thank you for...I'm not sure what. But thank you for your presence during that ordeal, Mr. Murphy."

"Not a problem, Miss Cooper. Unfortunately, not all of these men were taught by their mothers to be gentlemen. You should be on your guard when you're down here."

Evan couldn't help feeling a little smug, but he didn't dare let on. Instead, he turned to the man. "Evan Covington. I'm the attorney representing Mr. Franco Giovanni. I don't believe we've met. Do you mind if I ask you a few questions?"

"Seems everyone has questions for me today. I'll tell you the same as I told your friend here. My nets were cut a few weeks back. I lost a day's wages, plus the cost of new nets. I didn't see who did it."

"Do you have any idea who might have—"

"I've got me suspicions, same as everyone else. But I'll not accuse a man when I've no proof."

"Have you and some of the other men gotten together to keep watch at night?"

"Yeah. But whoever this is, is smart. Sneaky. We've not as yet been able to catch him. Problem is, fishing is hard work. No one can give up a day's labor, and by the time we're done with our workday, we're exhausted. So as much as we try, it's hard to stay up all night and keep watch. And as soon as whoever's watchin' starts snoozin', this fella strikes."

"I know the Rangers have been patrolling the area. But they have other areas to monitor as well. They can't be here all the time," Evan said.

Amelia stepped a little closer and spoke quietly. "What if someone could keep watch all night? Someone who wouldn't fall asleep?"

"Why, I'd offer them space in my rig if they'd do such a thing."

"Miss Cooper, I hardly think it's appropriate for you to—"

"It could work, Evan. We could both come down here. Disguise ourselves as fishermen and hide out. I'm willing to try it, Mr. Murphy."

"Oh, lassie. I agree with Mr. Covington. The docks at night are no place for a lady."

"But they are a place for a reporter. And if I dress like a man, no one will suspect..."

Nearby, a fisherman pounded nails into a crossbeam on a mast. Evan's heart pounded in time with the hammer. He touched Amelia's arm and leaned toward her. "This is not a good idea. I'm certain Mr. Thomas would not approve."

"It's not your decision. Tonight I'll be taking the night watch. You're welcome to join me or not, Mr. Covington."

He could see he had no sway over her decision. If he were her husband—the thought disturbed and excited him at the same time—he might have a little more influence. As it was, he was simply an acquaintance. Well, if she was going to follow through with this absurdity, he might as well do what he could to keep her safe. Why, he'd never met a more exasperating woman in his entire existence. And that included his sister.

Without a word, he held out his elbow to her, but she refused to accept it. "I still have work to do, Mr. Covington."

That's when he whispered so that only Amelia and Mr. Murphy could hear, "I'm assuming you don't have proper fishing attire in your wardrobe, Miss Cooper. If we're going to do this thing, we have some shopping to do."

There it was. The smile he loved so much. Only this time, its effects were tainted with his concern over what they might be getting themselves into.

CHAPTER 6

*A*melia sat on the edge of her bed, peering out the window and trying not to fidget. Why, she'd never done anything so deliciously scandalous since...ever. They'd purchased the smallest fishing attire the general store carried, which was still too big. But she supposed that was actually a good thing, for the bulk disguised her womanly shape and features.

Evan was supposed to be there at 10:15—all the other residents would be asleep by then. He would appear outside her window with a lantern and wave it back and forth three times. Then she'd sneak downstairs and out the door. And as long as she wore her hat and kept her face down, no one would question two fishermen out after dark.

The quarter hour came and went, however, with no sign of Evan. Where was he? What could be keeping him? It was now... seventeen after. Should she go on downstairs and wait for him there?

A dim light appeared from up the street. She watched as it moved toward her boarding house and stopped right in front.

Once, twice, three times it waved back and forth before coming to a rest. It was him.

Though she crept down the stairs as silently as a deer stepping through the forest, she felt certain the pounding rush of blood in her ears would awaken everyone on the block. The bottom stair creaked, and she froze, until all she heard was the steady tick-tick of the grandfather clock in the parlor. Cautiously she moved forward, slipping through the front door and down the front steps.

"I thought you'd never come," she whispered.

"I'm not that late, am I? I recognized a couple of men as I walked through town. They were standing outside one of the saloons, so I had to wait until they were occupied. I didn't want anyone to recognize and question me."

"You're fine. No need to apologize. I'm just excited."

"It is rather exciting. But I hope you understand the danger as well. I can't stress to you enough the importance of remaining incognito at all times, Miss Cooper. No story is worth your reputation or your safety."

"I understand completely, Mr. Covington. I just hope we can find out who's causing the damage."

As they neared the docks, Evan slowed. "Remember. You stay on Mr. Murphy's boat, behind those two barrels. I'll stay on the dock, near the supply store. Ideally we can find a position where we can see each other."

"Remember the sign language you helped me learn? If we see anything suspicious, we can communicate by signing."

"We can try. It may be too dark to see well enough."

"That's true."

"You promised to take notes and nothing more. Do you recall that?"

"Yes."

"No matter what happens?"

"I promise."

"Very well, then. Let's go get our man." Evan placed his hand on her elbow, but she pulled away.

"You can't treat me like a lady, Mr. Covington. Remember, I'm supposed to be a man."

"Oh, yes. Sorry."

Amelia couldn't remember a single person in her life who treated her like Evan did. Oh, he was protective of her. But he acted like she was capable and smart. Like her thoughts were important. Like her ideas and input had value, even if they weren't traditional.

It was clear he would have preferred she not participate in this investigation. But he didn't try to forbid it or bully her into thinking she was too delicate for such matters. It was nice to be treated as an equal. So nice, as a matter of fact, that she had to remind herself more and more often that a romantic relationship would never work between them. Though the reasons why it would never work were becoming more and more cloudy.

Mr. Murphy waited. When they approached his rig, he made quite the scene, yelling at her because she was late, throwing her a rope that nearly knocked her over with its weight and telling her to get to work. It was all part of the plan, so no one would suspect anything other than that Murphy had hired a new assistant.

She lowered her voice to its deepest timbre and uttered, "Aye, aye, cap'n."

That's when Evan left her and moved further up the dock. As she coiled the rope, she watched him and realized she couldn't think of a single reason why she shouldn't fall head over heels in love with Evan Covington. Even if she could have thought of one, it wouldn't have mattered. For she realized she was already in so deep, she was practically drowning.

～

*E*van made his way down the side alley next to the supply store. The place never really closed since fishermen were known to keep odd hours. But he'd learned from Murphy the hours between 11 p.m. and 3 a.m. were pretty quiet. Evan decided if he disappeared into the shadows a little before eleven, he might catch a glimpse of something.

He positioned himself where he could see Amelia, and he couldn't keep from smiling. It would be hard to stay focused on the task at hand with such a comical, adorable fishing hand just a few yards up from him, looking as much like a teen boy as any teen boy he'd ever seen. Quite the change from the feminine form he knew hid beneath the layers of cotton canvas and plaid.

He was ready to admit to himself the very thing Elizabeth had accused him of. He was in love with Amelia Cooper, and each day he was in a little deeper. But with what was sure to be a near-constant collision of their two professions, Evan wasn't sure how it would work.

She couldn't give up her journalism. Why, she thrived on it. Whenever she thought she was onto a story, something inside her lit up like one of Edison's light bulbs. Even when she worked on one of the society page articles, despite her protests about the shallow subject matter, she relished spinning the words on the page like...like a candy maker spun sugar. Like a potter spun his wheel. Like Rumpelstiltskin spun straw into gold.

The minutes ticked by. Her idea about sign language might have worked in daylight. As it was, he could barely see her now. The docks had seemingly gone to sleep, and without fanfare, she had knelt down behind the barrels and disappeared into the shadows there. Though he knew she watched, he also knew she couldn't see him at all.

Midnight. He could tell by the placement of the moon.

Nothing happened. Half past midnight...still nothing. One o'clock...still nothing.

And then, at around quarter after one, the slightest noise caught his attention. He looked to his left and saw a shadow lengthening along the dock but couldn't make out exactly from where it came.

~

*A*melia held her breath as she watched O'Riley move from one shadow to the next. She never would have guessed the hefty man could be so catlike, but there he was. Not a sound. If she hadn't been looking for something, she probably wouldn't have noticed him.

Then he stopped, so deep in the shadows she could just barely make out the whites of his eyes...and she wasn't even sure if she was imagining those. Finally he moved on to the next shadow.

What was he doing? Oh, dear.

Though she was certain the man was up to no good, she couldn't very well accuse him of doing something she couldn't actually see him doing. He worked down here. Slept on his boat, as a matter of fact, just as Murphy and many of the other men did. He had as much right as anyone to take a moonlight stroll.

Which is exactly what he'd say he was doing if she tried to implicate him. She wanted to look at Evan, but she was afraid if she took her eyes from the creeping form for even a second, she wouldn't find him again. No, she needed to follow him.

It was foolish, she knew. But Evan was here. If anything happened, at least she had a witness. Without a sound, she called on the same stealth she'd used as a child when she and her cousins played hide-and-seek after dark. She'd always been the last one found, and they usually had to call her out of her spot because it was time to go in. She remembered how her heart had pounded then, yet she'd managed to remain hidden.

Well, the stakes were higher now. O'Riley probably weighed two hundred pounds or more. If he could sneak around undetected, so could she. Without moving her eyes from him, she used her peripheral vision to step the short distance from the boat to the dock, hanging on to a post for support. Then, crouching low to the ground, she slinked from one shadow to the next, toward O'Riley, praying all the while.

God, I'm pretty sure this isn't a great idea. But someone needs to catch the man who's behind all the vandalism. Fishing is the livelihood for these men and their families. Please use me to help get to the bottom of this.

Oh, and if I get my big break as a journalist because of it, that would be great, too.

Uhm...amen.

As she passed the alley where Evan had disappeared earlier, her heart hammered inside her, but she refused to look for him. O'Riley had just walked onto the next dock, and she could barely make out his form ahead. But what was he doing? She had to get closer.

The nerves at the back of her neck stood to attention, and she knew someone was behind her. *Oh, dear God... please let it be Evan.*

Voices inside her head competed to be heard. One told her to keep going, to play this story out to the end. The other told her to hide, to retreat, to run back home to her bed at Mrs. Green's and pull the covers over her head.

She listened to the first one and did her best to muffle the second one.

Into the shadows she crept, forward and forward until she could no longer see O'Riley. He'd just been right here. Where did he go? She willed her eyes to see through the dark, but there was nothing.

Wait...there he was. And in his hand was a knife. He was cutting the rope that tied the boat to the dock. Why, some poor fisherman's boat was going to float away. The boat might not be damaged, but it would surely cost someone several hours of trying to get back on course. No telling where the waves would take the boat without anyone controlling the rudder. It could even crash into a rock. She watched O'Riley move to the next mooring and do the same thing. Was he going to cut them all?

He disappeared again, into the black. She squinted but could see nothing more.

Suddenly she felt someone grab her from behind. A meaty hand clasped over her mouth and nose until not only couldn't she scream, but she couldn't breathe, either. She kicked, but it was no use. She was kicking at air. The man had lifted her effortlessly and was now carrying her toward O'Riley's boat.

She tried to open her mouth to bite him, but she couldn't even do that. His grip was too tight. *Oh, dear God, please. Help me.*

"Hold it right there. Put your hands over your head."

The man froze, then dropped her—kerplunk!—onto the dock.

"Who's there?" O'Riley's voice spoke from behind her.

"This is Lieutenant Rett Smith of the Texas Rangers," came the voice from the dark. After a moment, a match flickered. Then a kerosene lamp illuminated the dock. Why, there was Ranger Smith, Ranger McCoy, and Sheriff Goodman, all three. All armed. Where had they come from? Evan stepped beside her and held out a hand. "What were you doing? That wasn't in the plan." His other hand was on his hip, pushing back his jacket.

"I had to get a closer look. Why are all these men here? Did you tell them?"

"I might have mentioned our plans to Rett."

Amelia didn't know whether to feel angry or relieved. She didn't want to think what might have happened if the lawmen hadn't stepped in. But she wished they hadn't. What a great story this would have made. Still would, she supposed. "It wasn't in *the plan* to share our plans, Mr. Covington. Nevertheless, it looks like we have our man."

O'Riley shifted his attention briefly from the law officers who were questioning him to her, then turned to face her full-on as recognition registered on his face. "You. I should have known you'd be behind this scheme to implicate me again. Why, you set me up."

She'd forgotten about her disguise. Taking hold of Evan's hand, she pulled herself to her feet. "You set yourself up, Mr. O'Riley. I am, however, glad I was here to witness it."

The man lunged for her, but Evan stepped in front of her as the other three men grabbed O'Riley from behind and placed handcuffs on him. They nudged him up the dock, where several sleepy-eyed fishermen watched, their lanterns lighting the way.

"There you go, Miss Cooper," Evan said. "You have your story."

"And you have your man. I hope this will clear Mr. Giovanni's name for good."

"It should." When O'Riley was far enough ahead that he wasn't a danger to Amelia any more, Evan gestured for her to walk with him. The audience now gathered in groups of two and three, discussing who had seen what and examining their own boats for cut ropes and other damage.

"Well, well. If it isn't the heroes," Mr. Murphy's Irish lilt called to them as they approached. "When I saw ye leavin' my boat, lassie, I wasn't sure if I should go after ye. I sure didn't see anythin' in those shadows. Yer eyes are many years younger than mine, though, and fer that I'm grateful."

"I'm glad we finally caught the man."

Murphy waved good night and disappeared back into the boat's cabin. Soon they left the dock behind them and headed in the direction of the boarding house with nothing but the moon to guide them. If Amelia hadn't been dressed in men's clothing, she might have soaked in the romance of it all. As it was, she suddenly felt self-conscious. Evan looked all rugged and beautiful and manly, and she looked like...like something from a traveling sideshow.

"You look adorable, Miss Cooper." Could he read her thoughts now?"

"I feel ridiculous."

"Good. Perhaps that will prevent you from performing similar acts in the future. You could have been seriously harmed."

"I know. Thank you for being there."

They walked in silence for a few moments.

"Why did you tell your brother-in-law? Were you hoping he'd show up?"

"I...don't know. Something told me things could get out of hand. The way O'Riley spoke to you yesterday...you might have heard an empty threat, but there's something sinister in his eyes. I don't trust him. Something—God, perhaps—prompted me to mention our plans when Rett came to fetch Elizabeth home."

Amelia nodded. She could hardly blame him for blabbing when the very Ranger he'd blabbed to had helped deliver the answer to her prayer.

CHAPTER 7

The next month brought a sweet sameness to Evan's routine, and each day confirmed more in his mind that Amelia was the girl for him. Monday through Friday, they shared lunch. Some days were filled with spirited debates about religion or politics or the latest news story. Other days, they passed the time walking through town or in the park, playing I spy.

Several evenings during the week, Evan would spend time in Mrs. Green's parlor playing charades or jackstraws with Amelia and the other tenants, or he and Amelia would enjoy a quiet game of checkers or chess. She was a formidable opponent, and it was a toss-up who would win on any given night. Sometimes they practiced the limited sign language she'd learned from her interview. It was quite entertaining.

Sometimes they'd share dinner with Rett and Elizabeth, and the two women got along fabulously. It was almost as if they were sisters and Evan was the outsider in the group. Saturday afternoons brought more variety. Fishing one week. Horseback riding the next. And on Sundays, Evan greeted Amelia at the boarding house, and they strolled the four blocks to what was known as the church district.

One Sunday, they'd visit the Baptist church. One Sunday, the Lutheran, one Sunday, the Methodist. Then they'd eat at Mrs. Green's and spend a while after lunch discussing the sermon or making note of interesting differences in each congregation.

"I'm so happy to see you've finally given in to courting Amelia," Elizabeth said on a Monday morning.

"We're not courting," Evan told her, though he knew it was useless to argue.

Elizabeth leaned her head back and laughed, a very unlady-like laugh. "That's funny."

"We're not courting," Evan repeated. "We're just two people who enjoy one another's company."

Elizabeth gave him a look that said she wasn't buying it. Who was he fooling? He wasn't buying it, either. "Well, I suppose it does look like a courtship. But we haven't actually discussed the matter, and I'm not sure how she feels. If I bring up the idea of courtship and she doesn't see our friendship that way, I'm afraid things will become awkward between us. And I don't want that."

"Oh, dear brother. You have a degree from Harvard, and yet you can be so—pardon my bluntness—but you can be so dumb at times."

"What do you mean, dumb?"

She stood from behind her desk and moved to the chair across from him. She took his hands in hers and leaned forward until her eyes were inches from his own. "She's in love with you. Trust me. Ask her permission to court her. You won't be disappointed."

"How can you be so sure?"

"Because I've seen the way she looks at you. I've seen the way she blushes when you smile at her. I've seen her face light up when you walk into a room. The two of you are more entertaining than a night at the theater. Trust your little sister on this. Ask her about a courtship."

Evan thought about that a minute but didn't respond. Instead, he left her sitting there and retreated into his office, shutting the door behind him.

$\sim$

"*Y*es, Mrs. Lewison, I've got it." Amelia scrawled the recipe in her note pad, but she blinked at the ever-so-brief light that flashed across the page. A sneaky glance confirmed its source. The tall, leggy man across the street held his pocket watch and pulled on her gaze with magnetic force. Evan loved to use the pocket watch to reflect the sun on her face in the most annoying and endearing way. It was their signal he was there.

While her interviewee checked her reflection in a nearby shop window, Amelia held up one finger toward Evan and gave a quick thrusting motion—sign language for "just a minute."

Evan leaned against a cedar support beam and smiled as if he had all the time in the world to wait for her. Why were the unimportant stories—the recipes, the fashion reports—the ones that took the most time? Oh, yes. Because the ladies she had to interview for those reports were all long-winded and far too obsessed with embellishments.

"Be sure to write that it takes two cups plus two teaspoons of flour. If you leave out the two teaspoons, the rolls will fall."

"Yes, ma'am." Amelia sighed a little louder than she intended. When would she get her big break?

"Well, Miss Cooper...I can see I've taken enough of your time. I'll be going now."

Oh, dear. She'd hurt the woman's feelings. The mayor's wife.

Not good, Amelia. Not good at all. "I'm sorry, Mrs. Lewison. You haven't taken too much of my time. I apologize for appearing distracted. It's just that I mistakenly scheduled another engagement. I didn't realize how fascinating my time with you would be."

The woman's face softened. "Oh, posh. I'd be itchin' to go, too, if I had an appointment with that handsome lawyer. Go on, now. Better not let that one get away."

Amelia felt herself blush as she smiled her thanks, and looked both ways before crossing in front of a leisurely paced horse and buggy. She squinted her eyes to block out the sun and get a better look at Evan. Good thing she couldn't see those laugh lines around his eyes until she got up close. Mercy. Those little crinkles made her go weak in the knees every time she looked at him.

"I'm sorry if I distracted you from your interview," Evan said, but the spark in his eye told her he wasn't a bit sorry. He pushed a stray blond curl from her forehead, and even that little touch sent a jolt of awareness through her.

"Distract me? I didn't even notice you were here. Oh, did we have an appointment?"

Evan held out one elbow, and the two sauntered toward Market Square. "Yes, ma'am. I have a lunch appointment with the prettiest reporter in town."

"Considering Mr. Thomas is currently Houston's only other reporter, I'm not sure how great a compliment that is." Amelia batted her eyes, enjoying their repartee.

The wind shifted, and the scent of something delicious wafted from Market Square. She took his arm, and they continued toward their destination, still encased in their own world despite the bustling around them.

Once in the restaurant, the waiter seated them in a private corner, as if by instruction. Had Evan reserved a quiet table?

Was he going to…oh, dear. She'd had a feeling he'd officially ask to court her soon, but today? If she'd known it was going to be today, she'd have worn her blue dress.

The waiter offered a menu, but she refused. Evan had brought her here at least twice a week over the past month, and she had it memorized.

"What would you like today?" The crinkles around Evan's eyes deepened again, and Amelia wondered if she'd be affected by them fifty years from now the way she was today. Because if he did ask to court her, if he did eventually propose, she'd say yes. Absolutely yes.

~

*F*or the fiftieth time today, Evan felt for the small book in his jacket pocket. He'd searched high and low for a book on sign language. Propriety dictated that he not offer—and she not accept—a gift of any kind unless they were officially courting.

Normally he'd ask her parents first, and he had written a letter to Amelia's father. Just yesterday, he'd received the man's reply. Yes, Amelia had mentioned him fondly in her correspondence. Yes, Evan had his permission to court his daughter, as long as Amelia was agreeable. Also included in the missive was a clipping of Amelia's article about his release from jail, with a note from her mother that she looked forward to meeting him one day. So today, he planned to ask her if they could make this friendship an official courtship. And if she said yes, he'd give her the book.

If she said no, he wasn't sure what he'd do.

He stroked his mustache, then his sideburns, a habit he'd developed in the past couple of months. He didn't know if he'd ever become accustomed to the extra facial hair. But considering his uncanny resemblance to a wanted murderer had landed him in jail and nearly gotten him hanged, he figured a strategically grown mustache couldn't hurt. Hardy's flyer and Elizabeth's description assured him that Evan's facial hair was much heavier and darker than the felon's. He no longer looked like the wanted poster, and most people had stopped staring at him as if he were some kind of carnival sideshow.

Focus, Evan. So far, everything was going according to plan. He could tell Amelia hadn't a clue...but she was catching on. The nervous flutter of her hands as she talked was adorable and uncharacteristic of her typical miniature bulldog confidence. Well, if she was nervous, he was downright edgy. He hoped he appeared calm on the outside, because inside he was about to explode.

What if she said no?

He didn't think she would. The connection between them was uncanny. Still, what if she thought it was too soon?

"I'll just have the fruit compote." Amelia's lips formed a distracting little heart at the *o* in *compote,* and Evan longed to kiss them. "Something light. I'm not feeling very hungry."

Amelia? Not hungry? Not a good sign. The girl weighed a hundred pounds sopping wet, but she never turned down a good meal. Of course, she also never stayed still for more than a few minutes, so anything she consumed was burned off right away. "Aren't you feeling well?"

"I'm fine. It's just..." There went the fluttering hands again. He'd planned to wait until the end of the meal to ask his question, but maybe he should do it now. Put them both out of their sweet misery. He reached across the table and touched her arm, and she immediately stilled. Took a deep breath. Looked him in the eyes, expectantly.

"Miss Cooper, I..."

"Yes?"

"I have something I want to ask you." He paused to clear his throat. "These past couple of months, with you in my life, have been incredible. I never knew there could be a woman like you. I admire everything about you. Your intelligence. Your wit. Your ability to turn a humdrum event into a page-turning story. I'd like the opportunity to get to know you on a more...personal level. I...I've been in touch with your father, and—"

"You've been in touch with my father?"

Evan pulled the letter from his vest pocket. "I hope you're not offended. I got your parents' address from Mr. Thomas. I, uh...wanted to do this the right way. I asked his permission to court you. He said yes, with your permission, of course."

Amelia looked dumbstruck. He couldn't tell if that was good or not.

"So now, I'd like to ask your permission. Amelia—Miss Cooper—may I have your permission to come calling? Formally?"

~

He'd done it. He'd really asked her. How many nights had she dreamed of this moment, and here it was, staring her in the face. Amelia looked from Evan to her hands, then back at Evan. A slow, silky breath helped slow her pounding heart, and she forced herself to savor every smell, every sound of this moment, for she wanted to remember it for the rest of her life. God really was a God of second chances. Proof of that was gazing into her eyes, waiting for an answer.

"Of course, you may." She meant the words to come out confident, self-assured, but instead they were hushed, barely audible. She wanted to hug him, but that would hardly be appropriate.

Evan let out a breath, and for the first time she realized he'd been nervous, too. Of course he would be, but that man certainly knew how to keep a calm facade. Had to. His job as a courtroom attorney depended on it. That flash of vulnerability in his expression gave her courage to brush the back of her hand across his hand. Not a hug, but the best she could do in this public forum. "Did you have any doubt?"

He took her hand in his own. Their gazes locked for what might have been an hour, but was probably only a couple of seconds, before he looked down and reached into his coat pocket. "I got you something."

He'd gotten her a gift? What was it? Jewelry? Surely not yet. She couldn't imagine what. Her eyes were drawn to a small book he placed on the table in front of her. Its title read *Sign Language for the Deaf Mute.* She felt her face stretch into a delighted smile, for that's exactly what she was—delighted. What a thoughtful gift. She opened it, and inside he'd inscribed, "To Amelia, with fond affection, Evan Covington." Below his name was the date.

She turned the page, and the cover page read, "For the use of Deaf Mutes, and for the amusement and convenience of those who wish to speak with the hand and hear with the eye."

She didn't know what to say. It was perhaps the most thoughtful gift anyone had ever given her. She fingered the opal necklace her parents had given her for her sixteenth birthday, knowing it was the only thing that came close. "Thank you, Mr. Covington. I love it."

Two years ago, she thought she'd never see happiness again, and look at her now. Yes, God was all about new beginnings. May the book in her hand and the man in her heart be a constant reminder of His goodness.

$\sim$

She said yes. Evan wanted to stand in the middle of the restaurant and shout. On the tabletop, even. The most beautiful woman in Houston, in Texas, in the world had agreed to let him court her. The circumstances that brought them together, awful as it was to be wrongly accused of being a killer, had led this stunning creature into his life. Now, here he was with a booming law practice and a gorgeous, strong woman next to him.

He couldn't help but chuckle at her childlike expression as she studied the book like a toddler investigating a new toy. "I'm glad you like it."

The waiter took their order and returned shortly with their dishes. Roast beef for him, the fruit dish for her. She eyed his plate with hungry eyes. "Oh, my. I'm afraid I spoke too soon. Now I'm famished."

He'd expected as much, which is why he'd ordered her favorite. "We'll share."

A million-dollar smile was his reward, and he moved his plate to the center of the table. He was so caught up in her gaze that he barely noticed the tall shadow that fell over them.

"Should have known I'd find you cavorting with the press. Some of us have to work for a living." Rett Smith pulled up a chair and helped himself to a bite of the roast beef.

"Be my guest," Evan told his brother-in-law, and he and Amelia shared a smile.

Rett shifted in his chair. "Look, I'm sorry to interrupt, but something's come up, Evan." He lowered his voice, casting a glance at the people nearby. "The other guys and I really need to talk to you in private, in our office, as soon as possible. It's kind of a sensitive issue, and we could use your help."

A private meeting? Hmm…"All right. Give us a few minutes and I'll be there."

Rett pushed back his chair, nodded and left them.

"I wonder what that's all about," Amelia whispered, and like that, the love-struck waif was gone. In her place, the relentless hound reporter.

~

*A*melia swallowed a too-large bite in an effort to hurry through the meal. Yes, she should take her time. Relish the moment and all that. But here was a story unfolding, and courtship or not, she needed the scoop. Sensitive stuff, he'd said. Important. Needed Evan's help. Man, oh, man. Her mouth watered at the thought of it.

Oh, of course she wouldn't betray Rett's trust and write about it. Still, she had to know. What was so important it couldn't wait until Evan was back at his office? Had they captured some notorious criminal? Or worse...had someone been murdered? Her mind swirled with the possibilities.

"Slow down there, girl. Remember, Rett invited me, not the town reporter." Evan's knowing look brought her back to the moment.

"I know. But I—"

"No *but*'s. Anything I share with you about my professional life must be kept separate. I'll do the same for you."

"That's right. Evan, you're brilliant. Don't tell me a thing. That way I'm not bound to any kind of promise, real or implied. If you talk to me as your—" she felt herself blushing—"as the woman you're courting, I can't write about anything I hear. But if you don't say a word to me... I'm off the hook and on the story."

"That's not exactly what I meant."

"No? Well, I'm right, aren't I? Yes. That's exactly what we'll do. You go to your little powwow with the Rangers and I'll ask questions later—strictly business, of course."

"Who says I'll answer your questions? I can't compromise my position as a respected lawyer by going to the press."

"Then don't fill me in. I'll sniff it out myself. This could be my big break, to get me off the kitchen page for good."

"Kitchen page?"

"Oh, don't give me that. You know what I mean. Recipes. Apron patterns. Table settings. I should be doing more than those kinds of stories on a regular basis, and we both know it. And this...whatever it is, it's something big. I can feel it." She slowed her chatter long enough to look at Evan. She wasn't familiar with that look. Had she hurt him?

Of course she'd hurt him. He'd planned this beautiful lunch, bought her a wonderful book, and all she could talk about was a story. What kind of a clod was she? "Evan, I'm sorry. The thought of a big story just got me all out of sorts for a moment, but that's not what this day is about, is it?" She placed her hand on his arm. "You've truly made me a happy woman today. The thought of being courted by a notorious criminal turned lawyer —" He smiled at her attempt at humor, and she continued. "I'm so glad you asked me."

"And I'm so glad you said yes."

The two locked eyes, and once again the world shrank to their little bubble. Wow. She was really being courted by Evan Covington. Officially. It was too much to take in.

"Finish your lunch. The sooner I go to this meeting, the sooner you'll be able to start your snooping—sorry, I mean investigation."

The smile Amelia gave him came all the way from her soul and stretched her lips as wide as she could make them. "So you're okay with it? You don't mind if I try to get the story?"

"I'm courting a journalist. I'll deal with it."

This time she did ignore propriety. She lunged across the table and wrapped her arms around his neck. "Thank you." Just as quickly, she sat back down, her face heating at the spectacle she'd created.

No one around seemed to notice much. Most people had already accepted the fact that she wasn't your run-of-the-mill society girl. There weren't many of those in Houston, anyway. One thing she'd learned...most people weren't nearly as interested in her as they were in themselves. They were too caught up in their own worlds to care much about some five-foot-two wannabe reporter. And her job as a reporter was to infiltrate those worlds and write about them. Whose world would it be today?

CHAPTER 8

*A*s they left Market Square, Evan nearly bumped into his sister. Actually, it looked like she was coming to find them. "Hello, you two. I was hoping to run into you. Well, actually just you, Amelia. If you have a few extra minutes, I thought perhaps you could stop by the dress shop with me. I need a new dress, and you have such lovely taste. I'd appreciate your input."

Evan couldn't help but grin at the two most important women in his life. Elizabeth, nearly a match for his own height, and Amelia, who barely came to his chest, made quite an interesting pair. Different in appearance, yet near twins in spirit.

"Thank you, Elizabeth. I'd love to."

"Where are you headed, dear brother?"

"I have an appointment with your husband. Not sure what about."

"Perfect. I was worried you'd be jealous because you're not invited to the dress shop too." Elizabeth took hold of Amelia's arm possessively.

Evan laughed. "As much as I'd love to go"—he coughed as if choking on the lie—"I'm actually grateful Miss Cooper has something to occupy her time. She's rather curious about this meeting."

"For a very good reason," Amelia said, ruffled.

"Whatever the reason, I'm glad I get her all to myself for a while. Goodbye, brother." And with that, Evan watched as Elizabeth whisked Amelia away, their skirts swishing. He shook his head as he pushed through the crowd. Women. Fascinating creatures, they were.

Cody, Ray, and Rett barely gave him a nod as he pushed through their office door. Ray sat at the desk, holding a brown folder, and Rett and Cody leaned over his shoulders, studying its contents.

"Have a seat, Evan." Ray's voice held quiet authority. Gone was the teasing spirit he displayed when the law enforcement business was slow. "Thank you for stopping in."

"Where's Miss Cooper?" Rett asked.

"She...uh...ran into Elizabeth. They decided to do some shopping."

The three men exchanged a knowing look before Ray looked directly at Evan. "You do understand that what we talk to you about today is confidential."

"Gentlemen, you have my complete and total discretion. Miss Cooper has her job, and I have mine. We both understand the rules."

"I hope so." Ray leveled him with a look that seemed to pry into his soul.

Cody pulled up two more chairs while Rett locked the door. Evan's heart sped up, and he worked to remain visibly calm. What in the world could be so private, they had to lock the door?

"We've been called out for backup to Lampasas, Texas. All three of us are needed. They've got a murderer by the name of Jess Pinkerton Cahill Hutchins—better known as Pinkie Hutchins—holed up in some hills west of there. He's got a whole passel of thugs with him, and they're smart. Whenever a lawman gets near, they shoot from every angle. Pinkie's gang can't get out, but they're well stocked with bullets, it seems. The Rangers need as much manpower as they can get."

"Sounds dangerous." Evan still wasn't sure what this had to do with him.

"Yes...it would appear that way. But they've called for support from all the nearby counties, and some not so nearby ones as well. I think once we have the hills surrounded, we can scare them out. Smoke 'em out, shoot 'em out, whatever we need to do. That man—and his cohorts—must be stopped."

"Well then, gentlemen, I wish you all Godspeed." Evan had a feeling there was more to the story. He wasn't sure he wanted to hear the rest.

"Thank you. This is where you come in." Ray leaned back in his chair and examined Evan as if sizing him up once more before shooting the cannon. "We don't want to leave Harris County without a Ranger. If word gets out...well, that's just an invitation to every ne'er-do-well for miles around to show up and have a party. We were thinking that we could choose a man...swear him in temporarily... let him wear a badge and a gun...just so the Rangers' presence is still felt in the community."

Evan wasn't sure he liked where this conversation was headed. "Sounds like an excellent plan. I'll be glad to help with the swearing in. I'll even draw up some papers to make it legal."

"That's not exactly what we had in mind."

Evan was afraid of that but decided to play dumb. "Oh, really? Did you need my suggestions for whom to deputize, or Rangerize, or whatever it is you'll do? Because I can certainly help you come up with a list of honorable men. At least, honorable from my limited perspective, considering I'm not a native of the area. I'm sure it will be important to place a long-time citizen in that role so he'll command the respect of the people."

"Actually, the man we've decided to ask is already well respected, despite his short time in our area. He possesses great wisdom and diplomacy."

"Really? Well, I'm glad you've found your man." Evan stood. "If that's all, I must be going. Good day, gentlemen."

"Not so fast." Rett spoke with the authority he'd used that first day many months ago, when he'd placed handcuffs on Evan.

Evan sat back down.

"You're the man for the job," Cody said. "The only man who's both respected and fit enough to at least give the impression you'd give crooks a run for their money."

It was true. All the long-time, well-respected Houston citizens Evan could think of were also gray-haired and pooch-bellied.

"But I'm not a lawman."

"Yes, you are." Rett looked smug.

"Not that kind of lawman."

"You don't have to be," Cody said. "You won't need to do much. Sheriff Goodman is here, and he just hired that new deputy—Brody, I think. Not to mention the local marshal. You won't be on your own. All you have to do is walk up and down Main Street two or three times a day, flash your badge and your pistol, and you'll be good."

He made it sound so easy. Evan knew better. "I'm not a gunfighter."

"You're an ace shot. Elizabeth told me so," Rett argued.

Elizabeth and her big mouth. "Shooting a target is not the same as shooting a person."

"You hunt. You told me." Ray this time. Three to one. Hardly fair odds.

"Still not the same."

The four men fell silent, except for the soft drumming of

Ray's fingers on the desk. After a time, Ray leaned forward. "We need you. We wouldn't ask if it weren't important."

Evan inhaled a deep, slow breath, then exhaled. He had a bad feeling about this. But given all these men had done to make up for their mistake last summer—all the referrals, all the high praise they'd given him to prominent members of the community in order to get his practice off to a successful start—he could hardly say no. "Only until you return?"

"Only until then. You have our word," Ray promised. "Then, if you want to give back the badge, you can. But who knows? You might decide you like the job."

"I have a job I love, thank you. And how long might it be until you return?"

"You could do both. You wouldn't be the first. And we're hoping to be back in less than a month," Rett said.

A month. "A lot can happen in a month."

"But it won't," Cody assured him.

With everything in him, Evan wanted to say no. Instead, he took turns looking them each in the eye, then stared down at the floor before lifting his gaze to Ray. "All right. I'll do it."

~

*A*melia tried to appear interested in the fabrics Elizabeth had laid out before her on the counter, but her attention wandered time and again through the window to the Rangers' office across the street.

"Honestly, Amelia, I can't choose a favorite. With your classic features, everything looks good on you. I only wish I could have my choice of all these patterns, but green looks dreadful on me, and pink..." She held up a length of the lacy pink pattern. "With my height, I'd just look like a giant circus clown."

That pulled Amelia back to the present. "Nonsense, Elizabeth. Every one of these would look stunning on you." Elizabeth laughed. "At least I got a rise out of you. Look, I know you're all mushy, gushy, head-over-newspaper for my brother—"

That made Amelia laugh out loud.

"But I need another woman's opinion. Snap out of it, little lady."

"I know. It's just that—oh, look. The door's opening. There's your brother and your husband."

Elizabeth dropped the fabric on the counter and rushed to the door like a cat after the last drop of milk. Talk about head-over-whatever, those two had been married for nearly three months and still acted like they were on their honeymoon. Okay, so maybe they were still in the honeymoon phase.

"I need to go, Amelia. Rett's leaving town on some business. He's being very close-mouthed about the whole thing. I have to give him a proper send-off, and then it's home to an empty house. Why don't you come by for dinner tonight? It will save me from an evening of tearful anxiety."

"Of course I'll come. What time, and what can I bring?"

"Make it around five, and bring nothing. I'll need to keep my hands busy after Rett leaves. I enjoy cooking."

"Five o'clock it is. See you then. And by the way, Lieutenant Smith will be fine. He's one of the best Rangers on the force—everyone says so."

The two parted ways, Elizabeth toward Rett, Amelia tracking Evan to his office. She knew he wouldn't give her any clue, but still. She had to try. It was fun, getting his goat.

He was just lowering himself into his desk chair when she breezed in. "So?" She pumped an hour's worth of expectancy into that word.

"It turns out, I do have news I can share." He smiled at her, but the eye crinkles didn't deepen.

"News about what the Rangers are doing? Did they capture someone? Elizabeth said Lieutenant Smith is leaving town."

"I can't tell you that. But I can tell you that you're looking at the newest Texas Ranger on the force."

What? No. She must have heard wrong. "Excuse me?"

"I've been appointed as a temporary Ranger while the others are called away."

Temporary Ranger. Called away. She didn't know what to process first.

"It's only for a few weeks, probably less than a month. They have to go away on an emergency—all three of them—and they don't want to leave Houston without a Ranger's presence. All I have to do is flash my badge and gun a few times a day. Easy as pie."

His words said one thing. His tone said something different. Evan wasn't any more comfortable with this than she was.

"Tell. Them. No." The words hammered out of Amelia with every pounding of her heart.

"I beg your pardon?"

"I said, tell them no. I insist." She knew she had no right. Knew she was out of line. But...*Oh, God. Please no. I can't endure losing someone else... Please, God. No.*

Evan leaned forward in his chair, then moved his jacket to the side to reveal a five-pointed star. "I can't. I've already said yes. I'm already wearing the badge."

"Give it back."

"Amelia, I can't. They need me. I gave my word."

This could not be happening. Not again. She wouldn't lose the man she loved to gun-slinging justice...a second time. Flashes of that awful night two years ago flooded her mind as if it was happening right now. The soft knock on the door. The sheriff's sad eyes as he delivered the news about her intended. Gerald, shot through the heart. Bled to death before they could save him. She'd sworn then and there, she'd never fall in love with a lawman again. At least not the gun-carrying, badge-wearing kind.

Evan was supposed to be different. What a fool she'd been. Of course there were no second chances. She was destined to be alone. If love were meant for her, God would have protected Gerald. God would have kept Evan from strapping that—there it was, peeking out from his jacket, secured to his waist—that gun to his belt.

She rose to her full height and took the sign language book from her reticule. "If you're wearing that, I can't accept this." She placed the book on his desk, turned and fled from his office.

CHAPTER 9

*E*van just sat there as if a boulder pinned him to his chair. What just happened here? Should he go after her? Of course he should. He hefted his weighty emotions to the side, pushed back his chair and chased her into the street.

"Miss Cooper." He flung himself through his office door onto the boardwalk. Several people turned and gawked, but he didn't care. He had to find her. Why couldn't she be tall like Elizabeth? Amelia's petite stature was easy to lose on this busy city street.

Where was she? The newspaper office was in the opposite direction from her boarding house, and he didn't know where she'd head first. He stepped up onto the bench outside his office door to get a better view.

There, pushing through the crowd and headed toward the *Houston Daily* office, was the petite blonde who'd stolen his heart, and who'd just now given back the token of his affection. Well, she might give back the book, but she could never give back the part of himself that he'd laid at her feet.

"Miss Cooper!" He propelled himself into the crowd, nearly

running down the Widow Franklin. "Oh, pardon me, ma'am. Are you all right?"

"I'm fine," the woman cawed, "but apparently you're not. Let me get out of your way."

With an obligatory nod, Evan left the woman in the street with a mental note to stop by her quilt shop later, maybe buy one of those fancy pillows she made.

It didn't take long to catch Amelia—his legs were longer. He knew she heard him calling her name, but she kept walking as fast as she could, chin up. He could tell by the way she bit her bottom lip that she was trying not to cry.

"Miss Cooper..." He placed himself in her path and put one hand on each of her shoulders so she didn't have a choice but to acknowledge him. He leaned toward her and lowered his voice. "Amelia. Please stop." He wasn't a fan of forcing his company on others, but he couldn't leave things as they were.

She stopped but refused to look at him.

"Amelia." This time he whispered her name, and a fat tear trickled down her flushed cheek and spattered in the dust beneath them.

"Please, Mr. Covington. Not now. Just...just give me some time. I...you know what happened to Gerald. I...c-can't go through that again. Please. Leave me alone."

Slowly he lowered his arms and stepped aside. She took a deep breath, brushed the tear away and marched forward like a soldier heading into battle. If only she knew the battle she left behind her, raging in his heart.

~

"Nice of you to come back to work this afternoon," Mr. Thomas grunted from behind his desk without looking up. Amelia placed the scrawled interview in front of him. "Is this ready to go?" He peered at her over those forbidding spectacles that Amelia suspected her boss wore more for show than out of necessity. Then he turned all the way around and leaned forward. "Are you all right?"

Oh, dear. Was it that obvious? *Do not cry. Do not cry. Do not cry.* "I'm fine. Why do you ask?" Her voice shook as she spoke, and she knew she didn't sound very convincing.

Concern covered his weathered face. He stood up, walked to the inner door and shut it. He did that only for the most private, most important interviews. "Tell me all about it. Off the record, I promise."

Amelia had witnessed his kind side a few times, enough times to know he was more bark than bite. But she'd always been the observer, not the recipient. Oh, not that he was unkind. Their relationship was simply a professional one. He ordered. She obeyed. He paid her.

So when his tone turned gentle and fatherly, it took her by surprise so much that she forgot to hold the dam shut, and before she knew it, she'd blubbered out the whole story while he listened and offered his hankie.

Finally, after she'd sobbed away nearly all her tears, she willed herself to look him in the eye. He leaned back in his chair, fingertips together, a look of such genuine compassion on his face that she had to glance away for fear she'd start wailing all over again.

A lecture was sure to come, about how a woman's place was beside her man and all that, about how she shouldn't throw a fit and stand in Evan's way of doing what he felt was right. She steeled herself, but all Mr. Thomas said was, "I'm so sorry. I do understand."

He was full of surprises today. "You do?" she asked.

"Of course I do. My father died of a snakebite. Cottonmouth. It happened while he was hauling water from our pond, to water Ma's garden during a drought."

Amelia didn't quite see the connection, but nodded anyway. "I'm sorry for your loss."

"It was decades ago. But to this day, I don't swim. I stay as far away from ponds and rivers as I can. I know it's not the same situation, but my point is this—when circumstances have broken our hearts, it's only natural to avoid those circumstances in the future. We don't want to get bitten twice by the same snake."

He did understand. "Thank you, sir, for that."

Nearly as quickly as it came, the fatherly expression shifted back to professional mode. "Take the rest of the day off, but be here first thing in the morning. We've got work to do."

"Yes, sir." Part of her wanted to hug the man, but she thought better of it, considered herself dismissed and left. On the sidewalk in front of the office, she paused to take a few deep breaths. She had to admit, it felt a little better now that she'd cried. Not her heart. No, her heart was still a mess. But at least that burning behind her eyes was relieved, though she knew her face must be red and puffy. She didn't want to go home, and wondered if it was too soon to show up at Elizabeth's. Yes, she'd go there. They could have a good cry together over some cherry pie. The bakery was just up the street. She'd stop and get a pie or three. Maybe they'd just skip dinner altogether.

Elizabeth was at the door before Amelia even knocked. "I saw you coming. I'm so glad you came early. I'm a mess. Rett won't tell me where they're going or who they're after. He says it's a secret, and he doesn't want me to be in the position of having to lie if anyone questions me. It must be really bad if all three of them are going."

The taller woman brushed away a fresh onslaught of tears and invited Amelia inside. "What are those, pies? Perfect. I have a pot of coffee going and was about to start dinner. Three? What flavors?"

"Apple, cherry and chocolate."

"I don't think I can wait until dessert. Do you mind if we cut them now? Sit right down and I'll get us some plates, and you can tell me about your lunch today. I heard Evan had an important question to ask you." She smiled a wobbly smile. "I need to focus on something happy."

Amelia seated herself in the overstuffed chair while her friend scurried around, pouring coffee in her fancy Boston china teacups, getting out matching dessert plates. She should offer to help. "Can I do anything?"

"You just sit there and let me serve you. I need to keep busy. What flavor do you want?"

A tiny Deringer sat on the side table, and Amelia's eyes grew round.

"Oh, dear. I need to put this away. Rett gave me a refresher course before he left." Elizabeth took the gun and disappeared into the bedroom. A moment later she returned. "Now, what flavor did you say you'd like?"

"Cherry, please."

"That sounds delicious, but I think I'll have a slice of the chocolate myself. I normally drink tea this time of day, but Rett prefers coffee, and I've started to crave it when I'm feeling low. It does have more oomph to it than tea. Here is cream and sugar, and one very large slice of cherry pie." At last, Elizabeth dropped to a seat on the near end of the sofa and took a breath. "Now. Are you and my brother officially courting or not?"

Amelia inhaled deeply but couldn't bring herself to answer yet. Instead, she took a big bite of the pie. That would give her a moment to think.

While she chewed, Elizabeth sniffled and dabbed her eyes with a lovely embroidered handkerchief. She blew her nose— quite loudly.

Amelia swallowed, then took one more long, slow sip of coffee. Yes, coffee had more oomph than tea, and Amelia was glad for the long drink of courage before she had to explain herself to Evan's sister. She cleared her throat, sat up straight and tall and tilted her head up to look at Elizabeth. "No."

"Excuse me?"

"He asked if he could court me. I said yes. And then I changed my mind."

Elizabeth sat back and placed both hands on her head. "I can't believe this is happening. What did he do? I'll kill him."

"He became a Texas Ranger."

"He—wait. What?"

"Apparently Rett and the others didn't want to leave Houston without a Ranger, so they gave Evan a badge and a gun. Swore him in. The works."

"I know. Rett told me. That's why you changed your mind?"

"Yes."

Elizabeth had the look of a codfish, mouth open, closed, open, closed. Head shaking, she said, "I...I don't understand. I..." Amelia saw the moment of dawning in Elizabeth's eyes. "Oh, dear. Honey, I'm sorry. I didn't even think about...why, you lost your...oh, my. This is because of Gerald."

Amelia's response was another fork load of cherry pie shoveled into her mouth. Who needed Dr. Brown's Miracle Potion, or whatever was the current rage in all the ladies' magazines? Sugar could do wonders for numbing whatever ailed the soul. At least until she outgrew her wardrobe. Then she might have to call Dr. Brown.

The two sat that way for several minutes, holding back hysterics with pie and coffee, until Amelia finished her piece and felt like talking. "I can't do it, Elizabeth. I won't do it. Evan knew..."

"There's no need to explain yourself. I'm sure Evan just wasn't thinking. Once he understands, he'll give back the badge and gun. They can just find someone else."

"You know your brother better than that. Evan gave them his word. Besides, the other Rangers are already gone. They can't swear anyone else in until they return. No, Evan's a temporary Ranger, though I have my doubts about the word 'temporary.' Something in my gut tells me this will end up being a lifelong commitment on his part. Gerald used to say, 'Once a lawman, always a lawman.'"

Elizabeth acted like she'd protest but didn't. Instead, each helped herself to a second piece of pie. They decided to forego dinner altogether, and laughed and cried and talked until dusk, neither coming to any grand conclusion about life, but feeling better for the camaraderie. Finally Amelia said it was time to head home.

They were just placing their dishes in the wash bucket when a tall silhouette appeared in the kitchen window, next to the back door. "Hello?" Elizabeth called.

The door banged open and slammed against the wall, knocking a china platter off the shelf. Both women screamed but fell silent quickly as first one man, then a second entered, pistols pointing straight at them. The men wore black cowboy hats, with red and white bandannas covering the lower parts of their faces.

"Keep nice and quiet, now, missy," the taller one growled at Elizabeth. "Do as we say and nobody gets hurt."

"What do you want?" Elizabeth asked.

"I want you and that hero husband of yours. That's what I want." The man's laugh was more growl than anything else, and Amelia shuddered.

"Look, Boss," the shorter one said, waving his pistol in Amelia's direction. "Two fer the price o' one."

"Yes, I see. Not what I was expecting. Where's your husband?" Boss spoke to Elizabeth as if Amelia weren't there.

"He's...not here. He's gone."

"I can see that." He jabbed the gun into Elizabeth's ribcage, and Amelia sucked in a sharp breath, though Elizabeth didn't react at all. Just looked the man right in the eye in challenge. "When will he be back?"

"I don't know." Elizabeth's voice was calm, but Amelia picked up on the tightness there. "He's been called away on assignment. He wouldn't give me details as to his destination or his return."

The two stood eye-to-eye far too long, Boss sizing up Elizabeth, Elizabeth sizing up her captor in much the same way. Amelia tried to figure out a plan of action, a way of escape. Boss blocked the back door. His accomplice blocked the front door. It would take too long to get out the window. What about a weapon? If only Elizabeth hadn't put the gun away.

Where was the knife they'd used to cut the pie? There. The wash bucket. If she could only get the knife out, they'd have a fighting chance. She inched closer to the bucket on the floor by the hearth.

"Please explain yourself," Elizabeth demanded as if she were ordering a servant.

"I don't have to explain myself to anyone," said Boss as he jabbed the gun further into Elizabeth's gut. The woman didn't flinch. Amelia moved another inch.

"But since I'm a nice guy," Boss continued—the shorter guy chuckled—"I'm going to tell you. Does the name James Weston Hardy mean anything to you?"

Elizabeth went pale.

The man laughed, a laugh soaked in evil and basted in revenge. "My friend Charlie was part of his gang. Now he's dead. Hanged in front of a crowd, and you and your husband are responsible. I'm here to make you pay."

Amelia knew the story by heart. She'd written every detail herself in *The Houston Daily*. When Elizabeth and Rett went after James Weston Hardy late last summer, Charlie was the one who found Elizabeth in the woods and dragged her to Hardy. Later, Elizabeth shot Charlie, and Rett was responsible for his arrest.

Great. Talk about making a bad day worse. Well, she wasn't about to just stand by and let a couple of thugs kill her and Elizabeth. In a show of great brilliance or stupidity, she wasn't sure which, Amelia pretended to faint, knocked over the wash bucket and grabbed the knife.

CHAPTER 10

*E*van strained to read the contract under the dim lantern light. He was too tired and upset to accomplish much, but there was no point in going home, either. He'd just putter around, then toss and turn all night. Might as well try to be productive, or at least distract himself.

The contract was for a local cemetery, privately owned by a prominent family. The cemetery had fallen into disrepair, and distant relatives who'd come to visit their ancestor had filed suit against the family for not keeping up with the property. Or something like that. After reading through the contract four times and adjusting the wording here and there, he gave up. His mind just wasn't on the task at hand.

He'd pass right by Amelia's boarding house on his way home. Maybe he'd see if her window was lit up. If so, maybe he'd...what?

She'd asked for time. He would respect her request. But it didn't mean he couldn't check to see if her light was still burning. It would be a lesser form of self-torture than trying to revise a contract that affected only dead people.

Downtown Houston was still alive at this time of evening,

but not with the type of company he was fond of. Sounds of raucous laughter and popular music wandered into the night air, and he listened for a moment to the lyrics. He wouldn't have minded the music—some of it, anyway— but he'd never cared much for the rowdy behavior and off-color humor that usually accompanied those late-night establishments. He'd visited a couple of them with some of his college chums but had never acquired a taste for that style of entertainment.

No, he'd much rather spend a quiet evening in Mrs. Green's lacy-curtained, flower-printed parlor. The proprietress of Amelia's residence provided enough presence to keep their company respectable but also had enough decorum to allow them their privacy. His gut pined for what he'd become accustomed to, what he'd hoped to spend a lifetime doing...whiling away the twilight hours discussing politics and literature and the latest news events with Amelia. His Amelia. The most fascinating woman he'd ever encountered.

Not tonight.

Just a few short blocks from Main Street, not a creature stirred. Evan stood on the corner and watched Mrs. Green's lace-patterned silhouette as she blew out the one remaining kerosene lamp in her parlor. His eyes drifted to Amelia's second-story window. Pitch black. He wondered if she was asleep.

He stood there for a while, hands in his pockets, like some love-starved pup longing for the object of his affection. Who was he kidding? That's exactly what he was. *Oh, God. I know You're with Amelia right now. Please tell her I love her. Please change her heart. The thought of living the rest of my life without her just plain hurts.*

He turned toward home, but for some reason, he couldn't drag his feet in that direction. Perhaps he should look in on Elizabeth. Yes, what was he thinking? Elizabeth must be worried sick about Rett. He'd go and check on her. Maybe even sleep on her sofa. Yes, that would do them both good. Just like old times.

A swift about-face led him back through the center of town, where a couple of local working girls waved to him from the opposite side of the street. Nice girls, aside from their profession. He'd spoken to them a time or two in the general store.

Only, he wished they were nice in a more respectable way. Wished he could help them somehow, but he knew that wasn't possible tonight. Not if he wanted to keep his own reputation intact. He'd seen Help Wanted posters about town for waitresses and shop girls. If they desired more suitable employment, surely they could find it.

Still, he made a mental note to speak to Amelia about possibly doing a story on them...maybe helping them out of their current lifestyle...that is, if Amelia ever spoke to him again.

He rounded the corner a few blocks outside of town to find Elizabeth and Rett's home. Even in the moonlight, he could appreciate the tidy, well-kept yard, the overflowing pots of geraniums on the front porch, the classic toile curtains Elizabeth had labored over and hung a week or two ago. Nothing like the opulence she'd grown up with, but his sister had never been much for pretense, anyway. She was happy and in love, and Evan was proud of her.

Oh, good. Her lantern still burned. He stepped lightly onto the porch and knocked. "Elizabeth? It's me, Evan."

No answer. He knocked again. "Hey, sis. Take pity on an old bachelor and let me in."

Nothing. Not a stir.

A cold wave began a slow rise within him, snaking its way up his spine and down his limbs, spiraling around his heart. Something was wrong.

Slowly he reached for the door handle and turned it gently. Surely it was nothing. She was just asleep. Probably snoozing on the sofa after a long evening of fretting about Rett. Why hadn't he thought to come sooner?

The door squeaked on its hinges as he pushed it open and made a long, shadowy wave through the front room before it came to rest. The cold swell turned his chest to ice. He forgot to breathe. The kerosene flame flickered in warning across an overturned chair, a spilled wash bucket, broken dishes...*Oh, dear God. No.* In the center of the room, on the pale braided rug, were several dark red spatters.

Blood.

"Elizabeth." Evan tore through the tiny house looking in every closet, every crevice for clues, evidence, anything that would tell him where his sister was.

His search was fruitless. The house was devoid of life, save that taunting flame of the lamp, as if it knew a secret but wasn't telling. A gust of wind blew, and the back door groaned open. It wasn't latched? Evan grabbed the lamp's handle, pushed through the back door, and examined the surroundings.

He couldn't see much in the dim light, but he thought he could make out the faint outline of boot prints. Two sets. Man-sized. Back in the house, he looked for something, anything that would make sense of all this. His eyes fell on the table—what was that poking out from under the fruit bowl?

An envelope, addressed to Rett. It wasn't Elizabeth's handwriting. He tore into it, careful not to tear the letter inside.

I've got yer wife. If you want to see her agin, meet me at Gable's Pier, outside of Goose Creek, ten o'clock sharp on Thursday night, October 20. Come alone, or she gets a bullet.

*T*hursday. That was tomorrow. The ice block that was his chest cracked open with the pounding of his heart. Elizabeth. *Oh, God. Let her be all right.*

He urged himself on. *Think, Evan. Think.*

Get the sheriff. Get the marshal. They'll know what to do.

Who else?

Amelia. If anyone could snoop out evidence, it was her.

His lace-up Madisons seemed to grow wings as he ran back into the dark streets, straight to the sheriff's office. "Come quick," he yelled at Brody, the new deputy assigned to night duty at the jail. "Something's happened to Elizabeth."

Fortunately, the jail was empty. Brody startled, as if he'd been near sleep, but pushed out of his rolling chair and followed Evan back into the street. "What do you mean? What's happened?"

"I'm not sure. She's not at her place, and there's evidence of foul play." Evan couldn't think straight, could barely form the words, for the mental pictures were too confusing, too painful. Surely there was a logical explanation for the overturned items, the open door, the spattered blood. But he couldn't think of what it might be.

He tried to give Brody details as the deputy followed him to Mrs. Green's boarding house. Soon he banged on the woman's door. He hated to waken her, but he needed Amelia.

After a moment, the night-capped woman opened the door, a candle in her hand. "Yes?" she squinted through the dark.

"Mrs. Green, I do apologize. But could you please awaken Miss Cooper for me? We have a situation that desperately needs her assistance."

"Miss Cooper? Why, she didn't come in this evening. I assumed she was with you. Perhaps she arrived after I retired. One moment and I'll check."

Didn't come in this evening? Where could she have been? Surely she wasn't working on another story after dark. Evan would speak to her in the morning about that. Except no telling where Evan would be in the morning. He had to find Elizabeth.

"I'll get the sheriff. We'll meet you at your sister's house."

Brody was already down the street as he called over his shoulder. Evan rested one hand on his hip as he waited and felt the gun resting in its holster. Conversation from earlier in the day floated through his memory, and irony squeezed his ribcage.

You won't need to do much.

Just walk up and down the street and flash your badge. Nothing will happen.

Now the men he trusted most in this world to find his sister were hours away, chasing some holed-up criminal while who-knew-what had happened to Elizabeth. Where was Amelia, anyway? He needed her.

Needed her, indeed. No time to dwell on that now, though. He required her detective skills.

The door finally opened again, but no Amelia. "She's not in her room. Her bed hasn't been slept in," Mrs. Green told him. "I'm sorry. I'll listen for her. If she comes in later, should I tell her there's some kind of emergency?"

The frigid block in his chest expanded into an Arctic iceberg. Where was she? He remembered Amelia's and Elizabeth's shopping excursion earlier. Had they made dinner plans?

No. Surely not. Amelia was just on a story. As the society columnist, she was probably attending some soiree and forgot to tell Evan about it. He'd just have to fill her in tomorrow. "Yes, Mrs. Green. Tell her to come see me first thing in the morning. Thank you."

On swift feet, Evan tore back to his sister's home to find Sheriff Goodman and Brody already investigating. Sheriff Goodman wasn't Evan's favorite lawman, but he was always hungry to catch a criminal. Evan figured he was the best man for the job at this point.

The sheriff looked at Evan, then averted his eyes. Not a good sign. "You were right to send for me, Mr. Covington. It certainly looks like there's been an intruder."

"I found this." Evan showed him the letter, and Goodman's

frown deepened.

The man's eyes drifted to the blood-stained rug. "I'm not sure there's much we can do before morning, but we'll certainly try. Brody, round up a search party. Mr. Covington, I understand you've been left as the Ranger in charge?"

"That's correct."

"I suggest you stay behind, then. Let Brody and me handle the real crime scene. Post yourself outside the saloon in case there's a fight. If there is, just show 'em your badge and fire your gun in the air once or twice. They'll settle down soon enough."

"You want me to stay behind while you go search for my sister? Not on your life. I'm leaving now."

"No offense, Mr. Covington, but you need to let law enforcement handle this. You've had no training. You of all people should know the importance of letting people do their jobs. If the Rangers weren't gone, I'd welcome you to come along. But we can't very well leave Houston with no law enforcement at all, so we have to prioritize. We're dealing with a real crime scene. You're the least qualified to handle this, so you get to stay behind."

"You stay behind. Or Brody. I'm leaving."

Goodman shook his head in exasperation. "Do you even have a horse?"

"I'll take Elizabeth's horse. She's stabled out back."

"All right. You can come, but at least wait for the search party."

"I mean no disrespect, sir, but time is wasting. I'm leaving now." Goodman had no power over the Rangers, and Evan was a Ranger. He ran tense fingers through his hair and looked again at the blood on the rug. Something glinted in the lamp-light—what was that? He knelt down, holding the lamp closer. There, peeking out from beneath the sofa, was a delicate opal necklace.

Amelia's necklace.

CHAPTER 11

*W*hen Amelia awoke, the whole world was rocking. Back and forth, back and forth. She felt for the sore place on her head and realized her hands were tied. What had happened? Where was she? She opened her eyes, but a flash of light caused the pain in her head to worsen, so she closed them again.

Fuzzy memories crowded her mind. Elizabeth's house, pie. Two men with guns. Had she actually tried to fight them? A jostling wagon...being lifted and carried like a sack of flour... She wasn't sure if she'd dreamed it or if it was real. But considering her current state, it must be real. Snatches of muted conversation surfaced in her recollection. "Why'd you let her see your face? We can't leave her behind now."

"Just kill her. No, on second thought, she might be worth more alive. Carry her to the wagon."

Even with her memory revealing a piece here, a piece there, she still couldn't make heads or tails of things. And her head hurt. The last thing that made sense to her was sitting on Elizabeth's sofa, talking about Evan. And that thought added pain to her heart.

Wait. Elizabeth. Suddenly she remembered the evil man called Boss. His friend had been part of Hardy's gang. He'd been hanged because of Elizabeth and Rett.

Amelia opened her eyes again and tried to survey her surroundings. This was no wagon. And that swaying...what was that?

A small round window to her left revealed a cloudy gray sky, and the unmistakable smell of salt and seaweed drifted into her senses. They were on a boat.

That smell didn't come from somebody's pond or freshwater lake, either. They were in the Gulf of Mexico. Had to be.

Where was Elizabeth? *Oh, dear God. They didn't kill her, did they? Please let her be okay.* She moved her eyes slowly around the room. Sudden movements only heightened her pain. There, to her right, was Elizabeth. Unconscious. But she was breathing.

~

*E*van rode through the night, through a light rainstorm. He didn't really know where he was going, other than southeast. Goodman had shown him on a map where Goose Creek was. Considering there weren't a lot of roads—or towns —that direction, Evan figured if he followed the beaten path and kept his compass pointed in the right direction, he'd get there. And during that long night, he prayed as he'd never prayed before.

He arrived about an hour before the sun.

The town of Goose Creek wasn't much more than a general store, a post office and a livery. At least there was a livery. The rain hadn't lasted long, and the place was quiet as he and Sugar rode down its short main street. Evan wondered how long he'd have to wait to find another horse. Or get something to eat. Even coffee would be great. The odds were not good. But not impossible, either. Somewhere deep inside, Evan clung to the hope that Elizabeth and Amelia were alive and well. Somewhere in the dark recesses of his mind he heard a whisper, a still small voice, assuring him it was going to be okay.

Or maybe that was just his own refusal to accept reality.

Not that any of it mattered. Alive or dead, Evan would find them. With or without help.

He rode back and forth past the livery a couple of times, trying to see inside, praying God would give him some kind of direction. If only Rett were here. Surely the Rangers had some kind of special tracker training that would lead them to the women he loved and get them both out safely. If only...

Evan stopped himself. There was no time to waste on "if only." Evan was here, not the other Rangers. And Evan had a Harvard law degree, for goodness' sake, and those weren't easy to come by. If he could accomplish that, surely he could outsmart some hoodlum kidnapper. He thought of the letter. Why, the man couldn't even spell properly.

On his third pass by the livery, he thought he saw someone moving around in the stable, so he steered the horse inside and cleared his throat to let whomever it was know he was entering.

"Good morning," Evan called as he climbed down.

"Mornin'. We're not open yet," a man called from the shadows of the far pen. A horse whinnied in agreement.

"I understand," Evan said. "I'm sorry to bother you so early, but I've been riding all night, and it's a bit of an emergency. I need a fresh horse, and I'll make it worth your while." He pulled out his money clip and held it in front of his chest.

A wrinkled man emerged into the dim light. "I suppose for the right price, we can be open."

"I need the best horse you have."

"For speed or endurance?"

Evan thought about that a moment, recalling the marshy bog they'd have to travel through. "Endurance."

"Abby, here, is as steady as they come." He gestured to a dark brown Arabian. "She's not fast, and she's not slow. But she'll go through fire until you tell her to stop."

"How about swamps?" Evan asked.

"She's used to swampland. Ya need me to stable your horse?"

"Yes, please."

The man took Sugar and led her into an empty stall.

They agreed on a price, and Evan paid the man. "Do you mind if I come back for Abby in a few minutes? I'd like to find some coffee."

"That'll be fine. Your best possibility for coffee is a few blocks up the road. Norma Rae's Café. That woman never sleeps. If the sign says she's closed, just knock on the door and tell her Archie sent you."

"One more thing. Can you direct me to Gable's Pier?"

The man scratched his head. "I can try, but it's not the easiest place to find." He continued on for several minutes, trying to describe landmarks and distances. At last he said, "That's about the best I can do for you."

"Much obliged." Evan nodded to the man and headed up the road. Ten minutes later, he was seated at a table drinking the best coffee he'd ever tasted in his life. He would've enjoyed it more under different circumstances, but at least it helped awaken him for the journey ahead. Norma Rae also fixed him a hearty breakfast—she insisted—and then charged him an arm and a leg for it.

"You do a lot of business here?" Evan asked as he paid the bill. He probably needed to watch his spending for the next few days, since he didn't know when he'd make it back to the bank, and he didn't know what he might need.

"Enough. Usually not dressed as fancy as you, though."

Evan cringed at the reminder of his highly inappropriate, sopping wet clothes. Maybe the general store was open now. "I wasn't expecting to camp out on the trail."

The woman's eyes widened as he tucked his money clip back

in his pocket, and Evan realized she'd noticed the badge. "I didn't know you was a lawman. Here, take this back. Breakfast is on me."

Now it was Evan's turn for wide eyes. "That's not necessary, ma'am."

"Yes, it is. You just put this right back in that clip of yours, and remember Norma Rae in Goose Creek next time you hear of a lowlife or scoundrel sneakin' through these parts. We have our fair share, and I'd just as soon they find another place to eat."

Evan did as she directed, grateful for the extra cash to purchase some new shoes. Boots, preferably. "You get a lot of criminals through here, you say?"

Norma Rae looked around, then peeked through the window as if to make sure they were alone. "You didn't hear it from me. But yes. We get 'em slinkin' in off the Gulf. They treat me perty good 'cause I cook fer 'em. But I make sure they pay through the teeth, and then I give my full ten percent to the church." She looked quite proud of herself.

Evan hadn't noticed a church in the area. "Where is this church?"

"It meets right here. My husband's the preacher."

Surprise met laughter in a choke, and Evan was grateful that under the circumstances, he still had his sense of humor. "How interesting. I have a question for you, if you don't mind. Did anyone come in here last night, looking for a meal?"

"Not a soul. Yer the first customer I've had since dinner yesterday."

Evan smiled an obligatory smile and nodded. "Thank you again for the breakfast. God bless, ma'am."

Norma Rae's smile stretched from ear to wrinkled ear. "You come back any time, Ranger...what did you say your name was?"

Evan paused. "Covington. Ranger Covington."

His next stop was the general store. The proprietor—a thin, bespectacled man who looked to be in his forties— eyed Evan suspiciously. "Can I help you find something?"

Maybe he should wear the badge in a more visible place, considering the free breakfast it had earned him. "I hope so," Evan answered. "I need some better traveling clothes."

"What is your mode of travel?"

"Horseback."

The man looked Evan over as if taking his measure—literally —and gestured for him to follow.

"You'll need some dungarees...here, these should fit. And some boots. Try some of those against the wall. I'm sure we have your size. As for a shirt...do you prefer plaid or solid?" The man held up a solid blue shirt and a red-and-black plaid that reminded Evan of something the northern loggers might wear.

"The blue," Evan said. "I'll take two if you have them in my size." The man added a second blue shirt to the stack while Evan sat on a low stool near the window to try on the boots.

The third pair was a perfect fit—brown Western boots. A perfect complement to his gun and badge. What else did he need?

"Do you have a vest?" Rett and Ray always wore their badges pinned to a vest, and Cody wore a vest about half the time. If he was going to play the part of a Ranger, he might as well dress the part, too. Maybe it would bring him luck, or help from sympathetic townspeople.

Amelia flashed through his mind, and he grinned an achy sort of grin, one that hurt all the way down to his gut, yet he couldn't dispel the smile. He wondered what she'd say about his new attire. He could only imagine.

Less than a half hour later, a new man climbed into Abby's saddle, right down to the bowie knife strapped to his left calf. This morning, a frustrated lawyer had ridden into Goose Creek. But riding out in his place was a Texas Ranger.

He spied an old liquor bottle in the alley next to the livery. In an effort to see if he could still hit a target, and to make a statement to his audience—Archie and the store clerk were now standing in their doorways watching as if he were some kind of big news—he pulled out his gun once again. Opened the barrel, twirled it. Dug some bullets out of his pocket and loaded every last chamber. Then he cocked, aimed and shot the bottle into a thousand pieces.

Unfortunately, Abby wasn't expecting the shot, and she reared back, sending Evan flying in an arc. It was either God's mercy or sense of humor that landed him in the public water trough. So much for appearing tough and rugged.

Archie just gawked, his lower jaw unhinged. The mercantile owner stepped farther out of his doorway to get a better look. A couple of customers had joined him on the sidewalk, and they laughed, but no one offered assistance. Evan awkwardly maneuvered until he was upright, brushed off his dripping backside, and remounted Abby, who waited with patronizing patience.

Next time he had to shoot a gun while riding a horse, he'd be sure to hold on tight.

CHAPTER 12

*A*melia couldn't tell how many hours had passed since last night. It was the next day, she was certain. Surely she hadn't been knocked out cold for more than a day. But the gloomy clouds out the porthole camouflaged the time. And the way the boat continued to wobble and careen, she felt certain a storm was on its way. Almost here, as a matter of fact.

She'd finally pieced together enough scraps of memory to figure out what happened. The men, breaking in. Guns. Elizabeth, fighting back, getting hit over the head with the butt of Boss's pistol. Blood. She remembered grabbing the knife from the washbucket, remembered someone stepping on her wrist until she dropped it, remembered the pain as someone yanked her arms behind her back just before…a tender spot on her scalp indicated they'd hit her over the head, as well. She recalled Boss wanted revenge on Elizabeth and Rett for their part in what led to his friend's hanging. Revenge was a powerful motivator, and given the circumstances, Amelia could think of only one force more powerful.

God.

Nothing in my life has prepared me to know what to do right now, Lord. Elizabeth and I need You to save us.

A sudden blast of wind blew through the little window as if to confirm Amelia's storm suspicions. The cool wind felt good on her face. Elizabeth must have felt it, too, for she chose that moment to open her eyes a bit and moan.

"Elizabeth. Can you hear me? Over here. It's Amelia."

Elizabeth's eyes slid in Amelia's direction. "What happened? Where are we?"

"It looks like we've been kidnapped. Do you remember anything about last night?"

Elizabeth struggled to sit up but couldn't. Her hands were bound as well. It had taken Amelia a good five minutes to maneuver into a sitting position against the wall.

"Use your legs to scoot toward the wall, and then lean against it. That's right. See if you can scoot a little closer to me." Amelia could hear the men moving around outside, and she didn't know how long she and Elizabeth would be able to discuss their plight.

Elizabeth did as she was told but moaned with every movement.

"Shh. We don't want them to know we're awake."

"I think I'm gonna—"

Oh, dear. She was nauseated.

At that moment, the door opened and a stream of light landed on their faces. Amelia squinted as she studied the large silhouette in the doorway.

"Yer awake. Good. We're almost to our destination, and I'm hungry. I assume you can cook?"

Elizabeth heaved in answer, and a loud clap of thunder played in dissonant harmony. The sky chose that moment to open up and heave its own downpour.

"Oh, great." The man looked disgusted, then let out a string of expletives.

~

*A*t first, Evan thought Archie had exaggerated the details. Gable's Pier couldn't be that hard to find. Now he realized the man had understated the difficulty.

What he needed was a boat, not a horse. Plodding through the soppy marsh was bad enough. But the mosquitos. He needed to suggest this place to the other Rangers for when they needed a criminal to talk. No need to hold anyone at gunpoint to gain information. Just tie them up and torture them with the pesky insects for a while. It was enough to push anyone over the edge.

Even praying did little to distract him from the pests.

*Lord, I need your—*buzz!*—help here—*smack!*—please.*

He'd been traveling that way for a couple of hours when he heard someone—a man—calling his name. Who could that be, way out here? Evan didn't know whether to answer or hide. He guided Abby into the shadows of a thick clump of cypress and waited.

"Evan."

There it was again. The voice sounded familiar, but he couldn't quite place it.

"Covington. If you can hear me, answer me, boy."

Goodman? Was that the sheriff? Surely not. Clicking softly, he eased Abby out of the shadows a bit.

"Covington."

There he was—Sheriff Goodman. Though he looked in the opposite direction, there was no mistaking the hat, the set of the shoulders, the pooched belly that Goodman tried to suck in when he knew people were watching.

"Sheriff?" Evan called. Goodman's head whipped around, and he sat up a little straighter in the saddle. His eyes scanned the area, and it took him a moment to locate Evan. The sheriff picked his way toward him. "How'd you find me?"

"It wasn't hard. At least not until I got into this swampland.

The good people of Goose Creek were kind enough to tell me which direction you headed. You dry yet?"

Great. Apparently the citizens of Goose Creek hadn't left out the tiny little detail of his water trough antic. "Dry enough. So, you comin' with me?"

"I think we'd be better off going back, getting a little boat. I'm not sure we'll ever find anything going this way." "I thought about that. But whoever it is will be expecting someone to come by boat. It would be better to surprise them on land. Besides, the letter said just one person."

"Then we make him believe only one person is coming. But if you're gonna do this, you're gonna need someone backing you up."

Evan felt better knowing he wasn't in this alone. "Okay. Why don't you go back and find a boat, and head toward Gable's Pier. Maybe pass by it in the daytime…is it wide enough for you to pass? Maybe try to make it look like you're just fishing or something."

"Good idea. Brody's meetin' me at Goose Creek. I've fished the area, and the pier itself is in a little cove. But I know a spot just outside the cove, where the land curves out, that I can hide and get a good view of what's going on. We'll drift by, maybe even dock a ways up and circle back around on land." Then the man seemed to study Evan, study his horse, study everything about him. "That Colt the only firearm you got?"

Evan nodded.

The sheriff untied the Winchester open-top rifle that was secured to his saddle. "You may need more than that. It never hurts to have a second gun ready. Here, take this. I'll get another back in town."

Evan took the gun and thanked the man. Goodman nodded, clicked, steered his horse around and plodded back a few yards before stopping once more. "And Evan," he called.

"Yes?"

"Be careful, son."

Evan watched the man go. The sheriff wasn't exactly a father figure. But the term "son" brought an ache for his own father, now gone nearly a year. He had to find Elizabeth and bring her back safely. She was the only living blood relative he had left.

And Amelia...he had to find her, too. Whether she married him or not, his tie to her was even stronger than the one he held with Elizabeth. His sister shared his past. Amelia...*oh, God. Please. I want Amelia to share my future.*

～

*A*melia watched her friend through the porthole as the boat rocked and swayed. At least Shorty—that was the name Amelia had given the short one, in her mind—had untied her, so she could better brace herself against the waves. Boss had tied a rope to Elizabeth's waist in case she fell overboard and then left her there in the rain while he took retreat in the cabin. So far he hadn't said much about Amelia. Just grunted and glared and dug into a box of supplies until he pulled out some hardtack. He stuck an entire biscuit in his mouth, and didn't bother to close his lips as he chewed.

That seemed to satisfy him for the moment, and Amelia shifted her gaze back to Elizabeth, wishing she could do something to comfort her friend.

A wave spit from nowhere, knocked Elizabeth down and sent her skidding across the deck and out of view of the porthole. A loud thud on the other side of the wall revealed her stopping place, and Amelia gasped. Would she get back up?

A second passed, two, three...ten...and there was no other movement from outside. "I think she's hurt," Amelia called.

Boss exhaled in a heavy snort, like an agitated bull, set his half-eaten food on a barrel and exited. "You women are a real pain in the—"

The final word was masked by the storm and the banging door. Shorty just kept shoveling hardtack in his mouth with little groans of satisfaction, and Amelia wondered if the man was aware of anything but the food.

More thunder, more lightning. Amelia stretched as much as she could to see out the porthole but couldn't glimpse a thing from her vantage point other than the empty deck. Elizabeth must have slid down in the other direction.

A moment later the door banged from down low, as if Boss were kicking instead of knocking. She opened it. Sure enough the man carried Elizabeth, unconscious, over one shoulder like a sack of potatoes. As soon as he had her inside, he dropped her. Didn't even try to be gentle, just released her to the floor where she crashed, limp and lifeless, in a heap. A gash on her head seeped blood, and the area around it rivaled a goose egg in size.

"You big oaf," Amelia cried. "Do you want to injure her more?"

Boss glowered, then looked at Shorty. "Lance. Get the little Chihuahua a wet rag or something so she can take care of her friend."

So Lance was his name. Shorty suited him better, Amelia thought. The short man did as he was told, while Boss just stood there frowning. Well, he could frown and froth all he wanted. She wasn't going to just stand by and let her friend suffer without trying to help.

She took the wet rag and held it to the gash. At least it was swelling up and not cratering in. That was a good sign, though with everything else that had happened, Amelia had a hard time finding any kind of hope. For the first time, she let the nauseating thought linger just a moment in her mind.

They could both die here in this place. What an awful fate.

"She'll be fine," Boss said as if reading her thoughts. "She's just knocked out for a while. Believe me, when it's her time, I'll make sure it's more miserable than a bump on the head."

Amelia sent him a scathing scowl, and Boss knelt down to her level. He put his finger in her face and laughed an evil laugh. Then he stopped laughing and said in a low whisper, "And when it happens, you'll watch. And then you'll die too."

"You'll never get away with this, you know. There's not a Ranger in Texas who will let this rest if you kill Rett and Elizabeth."

If Boss's expression was dark before, it was pitch-black now. "You're an annoying little pest, you know that? Maybe I'll just kill you first." He stood, paced back and forth a moment, his hand rubbing his whiskers in a show of deep thought. She knew it was a performance for her benefit. The man wasn't capable of more than a surface level of depth. Still, he was capable of murder. Of that there was no doubt.

"I should just do away with you now. You're disposable." Why couldn't she just learn to keep her mouth shut?

Now she'd have to figure out a reason for him to keep her alive. Without thinking, she blurted out, "I have money."

Where the thought came from, she had no idea. It was a lie. Would God punish her for such a lie? She didn't know.

"Money? What do you mean, money?"

She had his attention now. "I have lots of money. In...a bank. In Houston. If you'll let us go free, you can have it all."

"How much money?"

How much money? Oh, dear. "Twelve thousand."

"Twelve thousand dollars?"

"Well, eleven thousand, nine hundred seventy-two dollars and eighty three cents, to be exact. I'm very careful with my money. I inherited a sum from my...great-grandparents, and I've been adding to it every month for the last few years. I'd... like to start a business." She'd always wanted to start her own newspaper, so she added her dreams and a dash of imagination to the lie, to make it sound believable. Hey, she was a writer. She knew how to spin a tale.

Boss laughed, a cruel, mocking laugh. "You? Start a business? What kind of business? Did you hear that, Lance? She wants to start a business."

Shorty laughed too, but his laughter was more of the nervous variety.

It wasn't that funny. She'd heard of women up north starting businesses and being quite successful. Okay, so maybe it was rare. But that didn't mean she couldn't make a go of it. Except, it was all a lie. She had exactly twelve dollars and eighty three cents to her name, which is where she'd pulled the twelve thousand from. And the eighty three cents, she supposed.

Boss stopped laughing and looked out the porthole. "Unfortunately for you, revenge is sweeter than money. At least where I'm concerned. But you're lucky. I like to eat, and I'm assuming you can cook." He turned around, stomped to the door, then looked over his shoulder. "I'll wait until after dinner to kill you." Then he exited into the pouring rain, slamming the door behind him.

She didn't know if her prayer, more raw emotion than conscious words, made it past the cabin's ceiling. But in that moment, her spirit cried out for God. He would surely rescue her.

❧

*I*t started drizzling again, but Evan ignored it. He and Abby plodded forward through the muck while the rain got harder and harder. Finally he reined the horse in under the thick branches of a weeping willow and decided to wait out the storm. With the wind whipping the way it was, driving pellets of water into his eyes, he was bound to get turned around.

He climbed down from Abby, stood there in the torrential downpour and looked up at the sky as best he could. The rain dripped into his eyes and soaked into his clothes all the way to his skin. With each boom of thunder, he wanted to boom back in frustration. "Why is this happening, God?" he yelled at the sky, and Abby whickered as if wondering whether her current master was a madman.

Yeah, he would classify himself as getting pretty close to out-of-his-mind crazy right now. *"Wasn't it enough that I nearly hanged for someone else's crime? Now You've got to take the two most important people in my life from me? What, God? What are You trying to tell me? Whatever it is, I'm listening. Whatever it is, I'll do it. Just keep them safe, Lord. Please."*

He was on his knees now, not caring about the rain and the muck and the thunder and lightning. For the moment, all he was mindful of was God, as he listened with his inner strength for some kind of direction.

After a time, the rain slowed. He climbed back on his horse, not sure he'd found the answers he sought. But for the time being, answers or no answers, he had to press on.

CHAPTER 13

$\mathcal{T}$he storm grew worse before it got better. Boss had returned, dripping wet, and Shorty stayed inside the cabin as the little boat tossed this way and that. Both men reeked of sweat and tobacco, and Amelia found herself praying for calmer weather simply so they'd leave. She said little, and the men left her to care for Elizabeth. At least there was no mention of tying Amelia up again. Her wrists were still raw and tender from the rope burns.

After the better part of an hour, the pelting rain turned to sprinkles, and the thunder and lightning decided they'd had enough fun in the Gulf and found another place to play. Boss stood up. "See if you can get the little dog to make us some lunch. No, better not. She probably can't cook anyway."

Amelia resisted the urge to spit on the man's boots as he walked by. Instead, she kept her head down and continued bathing Elizabeth's wound with cool water.

The door slammed, and Shorty pushed himself from his barrel stool, walked to Elizabeth's side and stood there.

"She oughta be stirrin' soon. Trust me, she's better off asleep. She's gonna have one big head-acher when she wakes up."

"You've had lots of head wounds?"

The man grunted. "I've had my share." He went back to his seat again.

"Amelia?" Elizabeth's voice was gravelly and weak, as if the sound hurt her whole body.

"I'm right here."

"I had the strangest dream," she said. Then she opened her eyes and groaned. "It wasn't a dream, was it?"

"I'm afraid not."

Boss bellowed from the deck, wanting Shorty to come help him with the anchor or something. The man heaved a frustrated sigh and left them. No telling how much time they'd have alone, and now that they were both untied...

"Quick," Amelia whispered. "We've got to come up with a plan. Are you familiar with sign language?"

"Where you talk with your hands?"

"Yes. We don't know how long it will be until we can escape, so we need a way to communicate without words. I'm going to try and teach you the alphabet, so every chance you get, watch my hands. I'll draw out the letter on my skirt, then show you the sign. This is A." She drew an A on her skirt, then showed her the closed-fist sign for the letter A.

Elizabeth was a quick study, and they made it all the way to G before Shorty returned. He took his place back on the barrel and closed his eyes again.

They continued their silent lesson while the man napped, and by the time he stirred, Elizabeth had the entire alphabet down and they'd practiced a couple of words. Any letters Elizabeth forgot, she just wrote with her finger on her skirt. It was a slow way to communicate, but at least they were prepared, just in case...

Suddenly the boat shifted and stopped as if it had hit shore. Shorty opened his eyes and said, "Don't get too excited. We ain't gettin' off this boat afore sundown."

Amelia cleared her throat. "Uhm…can you tell me what time it is?"

The man pulled out a pocket watch. "Eleven o'clock."

A cutting frost bit through her nerves. If only she could get Shorty on their side. He wasn't all in, like Boss. He was the lackey. What could she say to win him over?

An idea snuck through the chill in her mind. She lowered her voice and leaned toward Shorty as if sharing a secret. Just as she'd hoped, he leaned forward in expectation. "Lance," she said in her sweetest voice. "I know you're not like Boss. I know you don't really want to kill us. If you'll help us escape, I'll give you the twelve thousand."

The man's eyes took on a hungry look, hungrier than when he'd been eating earlier, but he said nothing. Just harrumphed, leaned back, and shifted his gaze out the window.

~

*M*inutes turned to hours. The rain had stopped. Amelia never knew mosquitos flew in packs. In her office, sometimes a lone mosquito would buzz in her ear and distract her from an article until finally she smacked it into a disgusting mess on the page. But here, they were everywhere. Kill one and five more showed up in its place. Elizabeth was in a bad way. Oh, she was conscious. Her coloring was a strange hue of white and gray and puce, and Amelia was concerned that if Boss didn't kill her outright, this whole ordeal would.

Amelia needed to relieve herself. Despite the fact she'd had little to eat or drink since last night, she had to go. She'd held it the best she could, but she couldn't wait any longer. The best way to ask for that privilege? She had no idea.

"Uhm…Lance?"

"Yeah." The man didn't open his eyes.

"I…" Amelia lowered her voice to a whisper. "I need a privy."

The man snorted. "There ain't one."

"Well, then, get ready to put up with some pretty serious stench for the rest of the day."

Shorty opened his eyes. "All right. I'll see if I can find a can."

A can? Really? Amelia felt her face flame. "Thank you."

The man was gone only a moment. He handed her the can and sat back on his barrel. Surely he didn't expect her to relieve herself in front of him. She opened her mouth, but Elizabeth spoke first. Her voice was weak, but there was something about the way Elizabeth Covington spoke that commanded respect without seeming overbearing.

"Sir, I can see that in spite of our current circumstances, you have a somewhat...chivalrous nature. Would you mind giving my friend and me some privacy? Please?"

Lance sat up a little taller, as if stepping into a new role of gentleman and seeing how it fit. "I suppose I could do that. But just for a minute, mind you."

"Thank you so much," Amelia said as he opened the door and stepped through it.

It didn't take long for her and Elizabeth to both use the can, and Amelia knocked on the inside of the door. "We're done," she called.

Shorty reentered, and Amelia moved past him toward the door.

"Where do you think you're going?" he asked.

"To dump this overboard. Surely you don't want it to remain in here."

He reached for the can, and Amelia prayed he wouldn't dump it himself. She really, really needed some fresh air.

But then he looked disgusted at the thought of what might be contained in that can and let her pass. "Come right back, you hear? Boss is out there. So don't even think about trying anything."

Relief superseded the humiliation of the moment, and

Amelia pushed through to the outer deck. Boss scrunched his face at her when she exited the cabin, but looked at the can and continued whittling a long stick into a sharp point. *Probably intended for me.*

His gun mocked her from its holster. She leaned against the railing and held the can as far from the boat as she could, turned her face away and poured the stuff into the water. Oh, she'd never take an outhouse for granted again. Ever.

The boat was anchored in some kind of marsh, just a little ways out from a cypress-studded bank. Off to her left was a rickety pier. She knew she should get back to the cabin, but she needed this moment. Placing the can on the deck at her feet, she grabbed hold of the railing, closed her eyes and put her face to the wind. The breeze felt like a gentle hug, a reminder that no matter the circumstances, there were always things to be thankful for.

Please, God. Rescue us.

Something flashed in front of her eyelids, and she opened her eyes. There it was again—that flash. What was that? It almost reminded her of...

No. Surely not. How could he find them out here?

She searched the area just beyond the bank. Cypress trees pushed knobby roots here and there, creating miniature pools. A weeping willow leaned out over the water, and under other circumstances, she would have thought this place was peaceful. Something moved in one of those pools, and she focused in, squinting her eyes to see better. Two bumps peered out of the water, back at her. Slowly, the bump rose into more bumps as a long, scaly-looking creature climbed onto one of the cypress knobs.

An alligator. Good gravy, there were alligators? There went any hope for escape.

She swallowed the boulder that had grown in her esophagus and turned toward the cabin.

Flash.

There it was again. Boss was busy, head down over that stick, so she took a moment to scan the shore's perimeter again. There.

Out from behind a tree, just for a moment, there was Evan, dangling his pocket watch. Their eyes met, and he stepped back into the shadows.

Evan. Amelia caught her breath, but she felt like her heart would implode, and for the first time since this whole ordeal began she felt the need to weep. But she stifled a sob, coughed to cover it and tried to ignore Boss's loathsome expression.

"Get in there, girl. You've been out here long enough."

With one last look at the cypress that hid Evan, she made her way back to the cabin.

～

*T*here she was. Evan sucked in a breath and forced himself to remain calm, despite the fact that Amelia was right there in plain sight. Despite the alligator that seemed to stand guard, making sure he couldn't get to her.

He pushed back the urge to shoot the beast, dive in and pummel the oaf that sat on deck with Amelia. No, there were two men. Probably both armed. And he still hadn't seen Elizabeth.

Instead, he pulled out his pocket watch and carefully found the sun's reflection. Flash. Flash-flash. There. He had her attention. He watched her face, that beautiful, questioning face as she scanned the woods. *I'm right here. Look at me.* He wanted to shout, to jump and wave his arms.

Her eyes rested on the alligator, and then she turned away. *No. No, don't go. I'm right here. Look at me.*

He flashed again, and she hesitated. Turned. Searched the area again until...there. Their eyes met.

I'm right here, he told her in his thoughts. Her face registered surprise, relief, and he was afraid she'd start crying. He quickly stepped behind the tree again.

The next time he dared peer around the trunk, she was gone. Well, at least she knew help was near.

He leaned against the tree, his blood pumping fiercely through his veins, and tried to breathe. He'd really done it. He was a Ranger now, albeit with no training and against his wishes and better judgment, and he'd done it. He'd found them. He hadn't expected it to be so easy. Though easy wasn't exactly the best description of this experience...

Now he had to figure out a plan. The letter said to wait until dark. Come alone. But what now?

Goodman would surely honor his word. He'd be nearby, somewhere, come sunset. But Evan still had no way of knowing how this thing would play out. He peeked around the tree once more to get his bearings. The boat was still in the same spot, the man on board still busy. But something had changed. What was different?

Wait.

Where was that alligator? The water near him shifted, and he lowered his gaze. The surface of the water was smooth, with only the slightest ripple. But there, just beneath, was a log-shaped shadow, moving toward him.

Evan's blood turned to ice, and his heart struggled to pump. He froze. Waited. Watched as the form moved closer and closer. He had to do something.

There was no escape. Any direction he stepped, he'd land in boggy marsh, which would only slow him down and increase his chances of becoming dinner à la carte— or alli-carte, to be specific. And if he was dead or injured, the girls would have no one to rescue them. All this passed through his mind in a fraction of a second. He pulled out his revolver, cocked it and fired right between the reptile's eyes.

CHAPTER 14

*A*melia stepped into the cabin and tried to calm her hummingbird heart. She couldn't let on that anything had changed...at least not to Shorty. As casually as she could manage, she stood near an open supply box filled with kitchen utensils. An iron skillet would make a formidable weapon, if she needed one. When she was sure Shorty wasn't watching, she began spelling out Evan's name. *E-V- A-N.*

Elizabeth watched intently, but she looked confused. Amelia tried again, this time slower. *E-V-A-N.* Elizabeth's eyes darted from Amelia's hands to her face, then glanced at Shorty to make sure he wasn't watching. Then back at Amelia.

"Evan?" Elizabeth mouthed, without making a sound.

Amelia nodded, and moved her eyes toward the direction of the shore a couple of times.

Elizabeth sat up a little straighter, as if anticipating some big event. Her face was still green, and she looked weak. If they were given the opportunity to escape, Amelia wasn't sure her friend could get out quickly. And with the difference in their sizes, Amelia didn't know how much help she could be to her friend, either.

Well, there was no point in fretting about that now. She needed to be ready for when Evan made his—*Bang!*

What was that? *Oh, dear God. Did Boss see Evan and shoot him? Please, no. Please keep Evan safe.* But no...the sound had come from shore, not the deck. Had Evan shot Boss?

Shorty jumped from his seat and opened the door. "What's goin' on?" he yelled to Boss.

"I don't know. Get them women tied up and get out here, now."

Shorty grabbed the loose rope near his barrel seat and looked at Amelia. "Sit down. Next to your friend, there."

It was now or never. The way she saw it, she had nothing to gain from letting herself be tied up. She had nothing to lose by trying to escape. From what the men had said, she was disposable to them anyway. Elizabeth would be safe, at least until Rett arrived. If Amelia escaped, she could help Evan rescue Elizabeth. That would be better than Evan trying to rescue them both alone. Wouldn't it?

With a swift motion, she picked up a skillet and swung it at Shorty's head. She wasn't strong. The force was barely enough to startle the man, maybe give him a bruise. She'd better escape now, for if she didn't, it would not go well for her.

While the man grabbed the side of his face in pain, Amelia pulled open the cabin door and lunged for the railing. From the corner of her eye, she saw Boss come after her, but she was already over the side of the boat, splashing into the water, swimming for shore, for the place she'd seen Evan just minutes before. The water was cool, but the salt on her raw wrists stung like fire. *Please, God. Help.*

The distance between the boat and the shore seemed to grow further with each stroke. She heard the whiz of bullets above her, but she kept her head down, kept forcing her body forward until finally, her feet scraped the mushy floor of the bank. She grabbed hold of a cypress knob and hoisted herself out of the water, but a root caught hold of her weighted, dripping skirt. She was stuck.

"Get down," Evan's voice called, but in her panic she couldn't tell from which direction his voice came. She tugged with all her might at her skirt until she heard a bullet sing past her ear, missing her head by inches, from the sound of it. She splashed down into the water and flattened herself as much as she could against the tangled roots. Taking a breath, she allowed her face to sink below the surface and continued pulling and tugging to loosen her skirt. Unsuccessful, she lifted her head just enough to gasp another breath, and with it came the idea to just shed her skirt and leave it behind.

Sinking down again, she unfastened her skirt's button and allowed it to open up enough for her to wiggle out. In this case, propriety would have to take a back seat to self-preservation. At least her petticoats were still in place. When she was free, she began inching her way forward. Just ahead was a wide cypress tree. She'd stay low and take cover behind its trunk. Over her head, bullets whizzed and zinged. Where was Evan? *Oh, God, please.* There was the tree. With one final heave, she lifted herself over a massive root and splashed into the water on the opposite side of the tree, right onto a... *Oh, dear Lord. What is that?*

~

*A*melia. Evan didn't know which to take care of first—the alligator that slashed and writhed at his feet, or the woman swimming toward him, directly in the line of fire of the bruiser on deck. He chose to aim for the human ruffian and prayed the reptilian one would give up the ghost soon. Closer and closer Amelia swam. When the man on deck realized he was being fired at, he pointed his gun toward Evan, which was exactly what Evan wanted. Every bullet sent his way was one Amelia didn't have to dodge.

Finally she arrived at the base of the tree behind which he stood, knee-deep in water, but he couldn't help her. To stop firing, even for a moment, would surely mean death for one or both of them. What was keeping her so long?

He tried to cast quick glances in her direction. Was her skirt caught? *Oh, dear Lord. Help her.*

Bang! *Just take the skirt off, Amelia.* Whiz! *There. That's it. Now get yourself behind this tree.* Zoom! Pow!

When he was certain her entire body was sheltered by the tree's massive trunk, he hauled in his frame, his firearm and his chaotic feelings. But he couldn't relax yet, for there at his feet was Amelia, trapped by the alligator's massive form.

She was covered in blood.

He knelt and cradled her in his arms, trying his best to stay behind the tree's insulation. Was she hurt?

"It's okay. Amelia? I've got you. Tell me where you're hurt." Evan's words came out in a jolted whisper, though why he whispered he wasn't sure. The other guy knew he was there.

Amelia's eyes were open. She was breathing. That was a good sign. Now if he could just find the blood source, perhaps he could stop it, though he didn't have much by way of first aid training or supplies.

"Amelia. Please answer me." The enormous animal had stopped its writhing. It was still breathing...slow, labored breaths that mirrored Amelia's. *Oh, dear God. No. I can't have come all this way only to have her die at the grip of a swamp monster.*

She was caught again, this time her leg pinned under the gargantuan gargoyle like some scene from a dark fairy tale. How in the world? It must have happened when the animal was slashing around. Evan used both hands and all his strength to shove the animal forward. Barely a nudge. The gator just lay there, unresponsive, and he knew it was finally dead. Amelia, on the other hand, had begun shaking, and all the color had drained from her face.

He anchored his sopping boots against one of the roots and repositioned himself for better traction. This time, he pressed his right shoulder into the animal's torso and managed to propel it forward until it finally flipped over, belly-up, and floated for a moment before briefly sinking to the bottom, only to resurface a moment later. It was enough time to extract Amelia's leg from beneath the dead beast and gather her in his arms.

The shooting had stopped. He needed to check, see what was happening on the boat, but it was too soon. Instead, he lowered himself against the trunk, into the shallow pool formed by the tree's roots, and held the woman he loved close to his heart.

～

The next events seemed to defy reason, and Amelia almost left herself behind in an odd effort to survive. She'd landed on some sort of cold, colossal creature, and it squirmed and struggled beneath her. Somehow, its tail lashed her in the ribs, and as she grabbed her chest, the animal kept thrashing until it ended up on top of her legs. For a short time, her body fought and kicked and clawed off the mammoth, but her mind went to a place of singular focus that she'd never been before. Was this even real? After a moment, everything slowed to funereal pace, even slower.

Above her, she was vaguely aware of Evan. Tree limbs. Shooting. Leaves, fluttering in the breeze. Bullets. To her left, a water bug kicked and swam like it was out for a day of recreation. Not a care in the world.

Funny, she felt herself shaking, but all she could think about was that water bug and how much fun he seemed to be having. She remembered those days, splashing in the pond with her cousins, floating on her back and finding shapes in the clouds. Not a care in the world. Just like that bug.

She was vaguely aware of Evan. What was he doing? Oh. Pushing that thing off her. The water bug just kept paddling.

And then she felt herself being lifted out of the water, cradled ever-so-gently in Evan's arms, and that's when the floodgates opened. She felt them coming, and she did nothing to try and stop them. Just sobbed and sobbed, while she felt his gentle hands rubbing her back, his tender words hushing and soothing her. Later, she couldn't remember a word he said, only that whatever it was, it made her feel safe.

"Amelia."

She couldn't stop sobbing. She felt Evan's hands on her, searching, like he was trying to locate something. What was he doing?

"Amelia, I need you to show me where you're hurt. I need to stop the bleeding."

Bleeding? She was bleeding? She tried to regain her composure, but she just couldn't. She hated crying, and especially hated that feeling of being out of control. The harder she tried to stop, the harder she cried. Oh, sweet molasses. She needed to pull herself together.

"Amelia, honey. I need you to stop crying."

"I—I'm try-ing." Her breathing was coming in short, jerky little spurts now, and she tried to inhale a long, slow breath, but it was hard with the onslaught of hiccups that had appeared.

"Show me where you're hurt. Just point."

She made herself grow very still so she could pinpoint the source of her pain...her side, where the animal had throttled her. She lifted her arm and rubbed her other hand over her ribcage. No bleeding there.

Her wrists. But they weren't bleeding either, though they throbbed.

Other than that, she wasn't hurting. Just cold, and a little distraught.

Well...very distraught. Extremely distraught.

"I...I think I'm—*hic!*—all right."

Evan pulled a dripping handkerchief from his pocket and began rubbing her face and neck. She sucked in a sharp bolt of air when she saw the red stains there.

"Oh, my. I really am hurt. I'm bleeding."

Evan kept wiping. "No, I think it's just alligator blood. You're going to live."

Just alligator blood. He said the words as if it were the most natural thing in the world, to be covered in alligator blood. Something in the absurdity of those words, mixed with the fact that she was still barely on the edge of hysteria, caused her to giggle.

Then he laughed, and she hiccupped. Laughter, at a time like this, was extremely inappropriate, but she couldn't help herself. Under the circumstances, it seemed the only sane response. Or perhaps she'd left her sanity behind, and she was in a different place entirely. They carried on like that for a few, blissful moments of emotional reprieve, and then she laid her head on his chest and just let him hold her, there in the water, leaning against a cypress tree with a dead alligator floating at their feet.

Yes, it was absurd. But somehow, considering all that had transpired, it seemed the most rational thing she could do.

~

*P*raise God, he had Amelia. She was safe. But now Evan had no idea what to do next. Elizabeth was still on the boat...or was she?

"Amelia. I need you to sit up. Talk to me." Evan kept his voice low, just in case the waters could carry his words across to the kidnapper..

She sat up and wiped her eyes, but still said nothing. "Elizabeth. Is she all right?"

Amelia looked to be gathering her thoughts, and for a moment he held his breath. What if she told him Elizabeth was...no. He wouldn't even think it.

After a pause, Amelia set her shoulders back and looked at him. He'd seen that look before. It was a cross between a bull and a bear. "She's inside the boat's cabin, and she's ill. She's taken a pretty serious bump on the head, and the boat caused her to be seasick."

Evan nodded. He'd traveled by boat with his sister before, and was well aware of the effects the ocean had on Elizabeth's constitution. "But...she's okay? The bump on her head...it's not serious?"

"I think she's okay. She's got a pretty big goose egg, but those usually look worse than they are."

"Tell me who kidnapped you."

"It was—"

"Hey, Smith." Amelia's words were interrupted by a man's voice, calling from the boat.

"That's Boss," she whispered.

"Boss?"

"I'm not sure of his real name, but that's what the other guy calls him."

"Smith."

Why was he calling Smith?

"You may have that little blond Chihuahua, but I've got yer wife. Why don't you come on out like a real man?"

Wife?

Dawning seeped through Evan's veins like blood. Iron-fortified, life-giving blood. This man thought he was Rett.

Amelia's eyes widened, and she leaned forward, as if what she was about to say was sacred information. "It's Rett they want. He arrested one of their buddies."

Amelia and Evan locked eyes for an instant, understanding flowing between them. Well, all right then. If it was Ranger Smith they wanted, it was Ranger Smith they'd get.

Amelia moved out of his way, enabling Evan to stand. He leaned as far as he could to the edge of the wide trunk without going around it, and projected his voice toward the boat.

"What do you want?"

"I told you what I want. I want you to come out here and fight like a man. You're early...which shows me you can't follow directions. You've probably got a passel of yer chums on their way to back you up. Looks like we're just gonna have to settle this thing now."

Evan's heart pounded, and he prayed for wisdom. And courage. Courage would be a real nice quality to have right about now. "Show me Elizabeth. I need to see that she's okay."

Another voice spoke in a low tone, followed by some shuffling. After a minute or two, the first voice yelled out, "Here she is. Come'n get her."

CHAPTER 15

The gravity of the situation seeped into Amelia's spirit in slow waves. She'd had a brief respite in Evan's arms, but now...now the possibility that he could get shot and killed at any moment loomed heavy, and the thought curled its way through her limbs and up her spine, wrapping snakelike tendrils around her heart. This was exactly why she had to separate her love for Evan, the man, from her need for Evan, the Ranger.

She'd do what she could to help him rescue Elizabeth. After all, it was Elizabeth he'd come after. Why would he come after the woman who'd rejected him? And reject him she had...there was no other choice.

Oh, her traitorous heart still loved Evan. But that would go away with time. She'd just have to train her mind on other things. She'd pour herself into her work. Maybe even get a job reporting at another paper somewhere. Yes, moving to a new location would be easier than seeing Evan around town.

But they both loved Elizabeth, so they'd just have to set aside their feelings right now and work together to save her. "Boss is the sharper one of the two. Shorty—well, his name is Lance, actually—is pretty dull. He's the one who's guarding Elizabeth. Perhaps if we can distract him somehow, it will be easier to take out Boss."

Evan nodded. "I think I'm going to have to show myself. Sheriff Goodman is on his way. He'll pass by on the edge of the cove, then circle back on land. We need to stall."

"That shouldn't be hard. Boss plans to kill both Elizabeth and Rett. But he wants Rett to watch Elizabeth die, or Elizabeth to watch Rett die...I can't recall which. The man is deranged."

Evan's face grew pale for a moment as he processed the information. Perhaps she shouldn't have been so blunt. After all, they were talking about Evan's sister, his only living relative.

"If there were a way to separate the two men..." Evan ran long fingers through his thick hair, and Amelia longed to move a wayward curl off his forehead. Why, her thoughts played Judas to her resolve.

She dragged her eyes from the curl. *Think, Amelia. Think, think, think.* Then, she remembered. "They think I have money."

"What?"

"I told them I have money. I lied, okay?" Something in her felt the need to defend the fib, though she wasn't sure why. "Boss was threatening to kill me right then, and I was trying to get him to spare me. I know. Lying's a sin. But—"

Evan touched one of his fingers to her lips, and she looked up at him. Goodness, it hurt to look at him, knowing she could never have him.

"You did what you had to do to stay alive."

"Boss isn't interested in the money, I don't think. He said revenge was sweeter than money. Shorty, on the other hand, might be interested. I...uh..."

Should she admit to promising Shorty money that didn't exist?

"What? Tell me everything you know."

"I told Shorty, when Boss wasn't listening, that if he'd help us escape, I'd give him the money."

Evan nodded, but didn't say anything.

～

"Smith. What's the matter? You a coward? You tired of your wife already? Look there, sweetheart. Yer husband's right over there, and he's not even comin' after you. I don't much blame him."

Evan had always been known as a fast thinker, but he'd never been thrown into a life-and-death situation before. One false move, and...he didn't want to think about the possible consequences. He needed to make sure every move he made was as well–thought-out as possible.

He called out from behind the tree. "You're the coward. Holding an innocent woman... Let her go, and you can have me."

While he spoke, he noticed Amelia peeking around the other side of the tree, and he reached to pull her back. She looked at him, and he shook his head at her frantically. The last thing he needed was for her to get shot.

The man laughed. "Now, why would I let her go? Do you think I'm stupid? You need to come after her. I have a few things I'd like to talk to you about."

Evan heard more low conversation. Amelia struggled to see what was happening. He wished she would stop that. He tried again to pull her, but she jumped back and looked at him.

"He's got Elizabeth now, using her for cover."

Oh, dear God. Help us, please. Show me what to do.

"Come on out, and drop your gun."

Evan had to act fast. He leaned over to Amelia and pointed back through the woods. "I'm going out. When the coast is clear, stay low and head that way, a few hundred feet. I have a horse tied there. Her name is Abby. If you just mount her and click, she'll take you back to Goose Creek. You can wait for me there."

"No. I'm not leaving without you and Elizabeth."

"Do what I said." Evan spoke with more force than he'd ever used with either her or Elizabeth. It startled her, he could tell. Well, he couldn't stand here and argue with her about it. He had to get out there and take care of Elizabeth. To his relief, Amelia nodded, but still Evan worried. He knew that look in her eyes. Would she obey, or was she just nodding, with intentions of doing whatever she wanted?

Well, that was a battle for another day. Or perhaps not… depending on the outcome of this day.

He gave her one last look before he stepped out from behind the tree and placed his pistol on a flat root.

"I don't think so, Smith. Knock it in the water." Boss had his gun to Elizabeth's head, and it was cocked and ready to fire.

"Lower your gun first," Evan called.

The man lowered it, but only to her shoulder. Evan didn't feel he had a choice. He reached for his gun, and Boss's gun went back to Elizabeth's head.

"With your foot," he yelled.

Evan straightened, then gently kicked his firearm into a shallow pool surrounded by roots. He hoped he could find it later.

"Now start swimming," Boss called. "And if that Chihuahua sticks her head out from behind that tree, I'm gonna shoot her. Should have shot her when I had the chance."

Elizabeth had that look about her, part panic, part stubborn determination. He'd seen that look last summer when his sister helped prove his innocence. Well, she'd saved him then. Now it was his turn to save her. He carefully lifted one leg, stepped over the roots of the cypress and began wading toward the boat.

~

*A*melia couldn't watch. She couldn't stay here and watch Evan and Elizabeth die. But she couldn't leave them behind, either. Oh, what to do?

Well, she wasn't doing anybody any good just standing here, hiding behind a tree like some ninny. Maybe if she found the horse, she could ride for help. But didn't Evan say Sheriff Goodman was on his way?

Perhaps if she moved further into the woods, she could get a better vantage point. She lowered herself into the water and pushed the dead alligator carcass aside. Reached around the tree...rats. She couldn't get Evan's pistol. But Boss's attention was focused on Evan now. Staying as low as she could, she eased further around the tree and got the gun, then retreated. Boy, would this make a great story. Except no one would believe it.

Keeping her body as low as possible, she half crawled, half floated through the marsh, maneuvering over roots until she got to more solid ground. There. At least she could walk now and actually see what she was stepping on.

She found another wide tree and used it for cover as she turned to see what was happening. Evan was about halfway between shore and the boat now. The water was up to his neck, but he looked to be walking, not swimming. He'd probably have to swim soon. She wasn't sure how deep the water was there.

Oh, surely there was something she could do. Easing herself out from behind the tree, she watched. She was in the shadows here, and Boss's attention was focused on Evan. She knew she wouldn't be seen.

Where was Shorty? If only she were taller, she could see more. Behind her, the land sloped upward. Silently, stealthily she crept deeper into the woods, onto higher ground, all the while keeping her eyes fixed on the boat. Evan was almost there now.

Something moved behind her, and she nearly jumped from

her petticoats. What was that?

The sound of whinnying...Evan's horse. She turned toward the sound, searching in the shadows. There.

Oh, what a lovely mare. Too bad she had no intention of riding her back to town as Evan instructed. She had little use for a horse right now, unless she was going to ride the horse out to the boat.

Now, that was a thought. Could horses swim?

She didn't know. She thought yes, but...that's when she spied Evan's pack. Or more specifically, what dangled from Evan's pack like a beacon of hope.

A rifle.

Amelia had shot a gun only once before in her life. When she was eight, and her father and uncle had taken her hunting. Papa had actually held the gun for her while she pulled the trigger, so she didn't know if it really counted or not. She'd shot a buck, and Papa and Uncle Rick had celebrated and called her a hero, and Mama had cooked some of it that very night in a delicious stew. They'd enjoyed that venison for weeks.

But the feeling of killing something so beautiful had made Amelia sad, even if it was for food. From then on, she'd left the hunting to the men.

This was different. Amelia eased up to the animal, whispered in a lulling, hushaby voice and stroked the horse's mane. "Abby."

The gun was only loosely secured to Evan's pack. She had no idea if it was loaded. After untying it, she pointed it at the ground, away from her, then added Evan's wet pistol to the pack.

Voices sounded from the boat—she needed to hurry. "Good girl, Abby. You stay here. Ideally, this won't take long. And with any luck, I'll be back."

The trees provided shelter, and she moved forward until she found one that gave her a clear view of the boat. She lifted the rifle, aimed straight for Boss and waited.

CHAPTER 16

*E*van wasn't sure of his next course of action. His pistol was gathering rust in a shallow pool, and he'd left the rifle with Abby. At least he had the knife strapped to his calf. That was something, though he'd never actually done combat with a knife.

He waded as far as he could toward the boat, then swam the rest of the way, until the one Amelia had called Shorty lowered a rope ladder to him. Step by sopping step, he climbed on board, certain that each pace took him closer to impending disaster.

"So you're a man after all. I'm impressed." Boss had a steely glint in his eye that verified what Amelia had said. The man was deranged.

"What do you want with us?" Evan asked. He stood close to the railing. Perhaps, if he could get Elizabeth away from that man, they could both jump. But that still left the problem of the alligators.

"Patience, Ranger Smith. All in good time." Boss nudged Elizabeth toward the cabin. "Lance, bring our new friend, here, in and offer him a seat."

Shorty shrugged, then nodded toward the door where Boss and Elizabeth had just disappeared.

Evan entered, taking in every detail. Boss still had Elizabeth in front of him, the gun resting on her collarbone. Boy, Amelia hadn't exaggerated. That bump on her forehead looked nasty. The swelling was emphasized by the rainbow of blue and purple and green bruising that invaded her left eye area. Other than the bruise, Elizabeth's color looked pale and drained, and Evan worried whether she could make it to shore, even if he got her off the boat. Shorty had a gun, as well, though his was still holstered.

If he could just get that gun away from Boss...or get hold of Shorty's gun...

"Sit down, Ranger. I'd like to tell you a little story." Boss gestured toward a barrel, and Shorty stepped aside so Evan could sit down. "This is a story about one of my oldest friends. His name is Charlie. I believe you and your wife, here, have met him."

Evan didn't respond. He searched through his mental files for the name Charlie. Best to keep a straight face, or the man might figure out he wasn't really Rett. Charlie... Charlie. There was a Charlie connected to the James Weston Hardy case...

"He's dead now. Hanged. And I don't like it when my friends get hanged."

Evan cleared his throat. "I...uhm...I'm sorry for your loss." He knew it sounded ridiculous, but he needed to keep the man talking. "How did the two of you become friends?"

"He took me in when I had no one. I was twelve and on the streets. Charlie wasn't much older—fifteen—and he looked out for me. We looked out for each other. By ourselves, we weren't much. But together, we figured out how to get by. He made sure I was well-fed, and that I had a blanket to sleep under when it was cold."

The man paused, and Evan wasn't certain if he should respond, so he said nothing.

"Charlie was the only family I had. Now he's gone, and it's your fault, Ranger. Yours and your wife's."

Evan thought out his next words before speaking. "I understand. I know what it's like to lose someone you love." He looked at Elizabeth then, and a single tear rolled down her cheek.

Boss stiffened. "Then you understand why I have to kill both of you. You're responsible for his death. I must avenge that death."

Words were dangerous things. Evan knew he must tread lightly. "It sounds like Charlie cared for you very much. Like he protected you."

"Yes he did."

"If that's the case, he would want to protect you now. If you kill us, you'll be a hunted man. There won't be a place in this state, in the entire country, you'll be able to go without your face haunting you from a Wanted poster. Charlie wouldn't choose that for you."

"You don't know what Charlie would choose."

"It sounds to me like you were both just a couple of kids, looking for a better life. You needed to feel safe and cared for, just like anybody else."

Boss nodded, but his jaw was clenched tight.

"If you kill us, you'll never feel safe again. If he loved you like a brother, and it sounds like he did, he'd want better for you."

"What he'd want is revenge. And that's what's about to happen here. Since yer wife is the one who shot him in the first place, I'm gonna make her suffer the most. If she hadn't wounded him, he wouldn't have gotten caught." He lowered his gun from Elizabeth's shoulder, cocked it and aimed it directly at Evan. "I'm gonna make her watch as you die."

Elizabeth, who had remained silent during this entire

exchange, opened her mouth wide and bit down hard on Boss's arm. He yelped in surprise but used his other arm to tighten his grip on her.

"Run, Evan," she yelled.

Evan stood up, grabbed a nearby crate, and swung it toward Boss just as the gun went off. A stinging burn sliced through his right leg, just below his calf, exploding in pain. A fraction of a second later, Shorty grabbed him from behind, but Evan jabbed him in the gut hard with his elbow.

He had to draw them back outside. That was their only chance—to jump overboard. Unless...unless he could get Shorty's gun. That would level things out a bit.

Boss still grappled with Elizabeth, who looked to be holding her own for the time being. Shorty was in the doorway, still doubled over from the gut-punch, and Evan lunged for him, knocking him onto the outer deck.

What the short man didn't have in brute strength, though, he made up for in heft. As they struggled, Evan found himself beneath the man's girth. As Shorty grappled to pin Evan to the ground, Evan reached for Shorty's holster and withdrew the gun. The look of surprise on the man's face when Evan cocked the pistol and held it to Shorty's chest brought both pity and triumph to Evan's conscience.

"Amelia told me you're not like that other guy in there," Evan said in a low voice. "Help us escape, and I'll make sure justice goes easy on you."

"Why should I believe you?" Shorty asked, and Evan struggled to get from beneath the man.

"Because I could shoot you now if I wanted. But I'm not."

"She said she had money. I could use that money to build a little house, start a new life..."

Oh, mercy. Evan wished the man would get off him. He was having trouble breathing. Inside the cabin, he heard Elizabeth struggling. He waved the pistol in front of Shorty's face, as if to remind him he was there. For just an instant, Shorty shifted his weight. It was long enough, though. Evan scooted to the side and scrambled to his feet. The man grabbed for his foot to try and trip him, and Evan reacted by hitting him in the head with the butt of the gun. There. That should keep him still for a while.

He could hear the stilted conversation inside better now. "Who is Evan? Why did you call him Evan?"

"You must have misheard me," Elizabeth replied.

"I heard you perfectly. That feller ain't your husband, is it? Evan...ain't that the name of the feller they mistook fer—hey, wait a minute. That's your brother, not your husband."

Evan had noticed a porthole in the cabin. As quickly and quietly as possible, considering his throbbing leg, he moved around the side of the cabin to the small, round window and tried to see what was going on inside without being seen. His leg was bleeding, but at least he could still walk.

He caught a glimpse inside just in time to see Boss pushing Elizabeth out the door, where Evan had just been. "Hey, Evan. Where'd you go?"

Evan watched from behind as Boss yelled at the empty gulf air in front of him. Then he spoke to Elizabeth, whose arms he had twisted behind her back. "Looks like yer brother jumped ship, missie. Aww, that's okay. I didn't want him anyway. My mistake." Then, to the air again, in a raised voice, "You have five hours. If you want to see your sister alive, you'd better go find her husband. If the real Rett Smith ain't standing on this deck at ten o'clock, she's done."

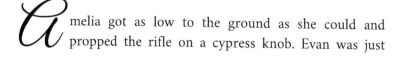

*A*melia got as low to the ground as she could and propped the rifle on a cypress knob. Evan was just stepping over the railing, dripping water behind, when she got the gun sighted in. Should she shoot?

No. She wasn't a good enough shot. Elizabeth was right there. But the minute she had a clear shot, she was ready to pull that trigger.

They were discussing something now, but she couldn't make out the words. Talk about feeling helpless...wait. They were going in the cabin.

Bzzzzz. Bzzzzz. Those blasted mosquitoes were even worse here than on the boat. And added to them were the most enormous flies she'd ever seen. Blowflies, she thought they were called. She tried to remain still, but after two or three minutes of watching the closed cabin door, she gave up and swatted the pesky critters away. At that point, she caught a glimpse of that dead alligator. Oh, cornbread. It had floated nearer to her, and its mouth was open.

That explained the flies.

Just then, she heard a scuttle in the boat and turned her attention that way once again.

Kaboom. A gun fired. The boat rocked from whatever was going on inside that cabin. Her rifle was aimed and ready to shoot when the cabin door burst open, and a flash later, Evan and Shorty came tumbling through. More scuttle, and it looked like Shorty had Evan pinned to the deck. She sighted in on Shorty. Could she shoot a person? She'd have to. She held her breath and pulled the trigger.

Click.

What? She knew there were bullets. Maybe it was just set at an empty chamber.

She sat up, back against the tree, and tried not to think about what might be happening on the boat. Tried to ignore the wide-mouthed alligator with the nasty flies, bobbing up and down on the waves, whose teeth were now caught in the lace of her petticoat. Tried to ignore the mosquitoes that would not give her a moment's peace. To the best of her ability, she focused her whole attention on the gun, on opening the chamber and examining its contents.

She cocked the rifle. Nothing. Cocked it again. Sure enough, a bullet moved into place. Little had she known, all those years she watched her father and uncle with their guns, that she'd one day use that information. Somehow, she'd thought being a writer was a gentle profession, and she'd fight her battles with a pencil and notepad. Funny how things worked out.

She rolled back onto her belly, but now Evan was alone, on this side of the cabin. And he was bleeding. His leg—oh!— Amelia caught her breath as old fears pushed their way to the surface. She couldn't think about all that now. She might be the only thing standing between Evan and death. Elizabeth, too.

Breathe in, breathe out. Breathe in... She forced her anxiety to the pit of her stomach, where she knew she'd pay for it later, forced her clarity and focus to the forefront. Shorty had his head in his hands, and Boss stood in the cabin doorway, holding Elizabeth at gunpoint and bellowing Evan's name.

Evan's name. He knew it was Evan and not Rett? How did that happen? She willed her thundering heart to still so she could make out Boss's words. "If you want to see your sister alive, you'd better go find her husband."

Find Rett? But that was impossible. He was away on assignment to who-knew-where? She sighted the gun in on Shorty but wasn't sure she should shoot the man. That would only upset Boss more and cause him to harm Elizabeth. If only...

Evan was looking her way, searching the tree line. She needed to let him know she was still here, without being seen by Boss or Shorty. With as much stealth as she could muster, she slowly, silently lifted herself onto her knees, staying close to the tree.

There. He'd seen her. Without thinking, she began speaking to him in sign language. Praise God, she'd taught him the little she knew. Though stilted, it was enough for them to communicate without sound.

"W-h-a-t s-h-o-u-l-d I d-o?"

"G-e-t r-i-f-l-e f-r-o-m h-o-r-s-e," he signed back.

Slowly she lowered herself, grabbed the rifle and held it up.

"G-o-o-d. G-o u-p-s-h-o-r-e. M-e-e-t G-o-o-d-m-a-n." Amelia thought about that. What would happen then?

Never mind. The sheriff would surely have an idea how to proceed. But… "W-h-a-t a-b-o-u-t y-o-u-r l-e-g?"

"I-a-m-f-i-n-e. G-o!" He followed the word "Go" with a desperate point upshore as if to hurry her along.

Well, there wasn't much more she could do here. She lowered herself again, then remembered her skirt, which was still caught on the tree root. Perhaps she could…there. She tugged hard, and it ripped. But a ripped skirt was better than wandering around with only a petticoat. She gathered the wet cotton and held it close, bid an anxious farewell to the toothy carcass, and crept as quietly as possible back to Abby.

The horse whickered as she approached, as if to ask, "What took you so long?" After settling herself into her skirt, then into the saddle, Amelia smoothed her fallen hair with her fingers, and twisted and tied two strands back from her face to keep it out of her eyes. Then she steered the horse in the direction Evan had pointed. She'd stay in the shadows until she was clear of the boat, then move closer to the water. She hoped she could find the sheriff before something dire happened.

Oh, dear God. This is insane. Please, God. Please protect Evan and Elizabeth. Show me what to do. And please, don't let me be too late.

CHAPTER 17

At least Evan knew Amelia was safe. For now, anyway. If he could just get Elizabeth away from Boss, perhaps he could actually make an arrest. Although the women's safety was more important than an arrest at this point. But if he didn't stop these two once and for all, they'd simply return. Boss seemed pretty set on revenge.

He didn't know how long he could hide out like this—the boat wasn't that big. And the longer he crouched, the more his leg throbbed. The blood had soaked through his denims now. How long 'til dark?

He had to get himself to shore. But he was weak, he wasn't certain he could make it there. Yet if he stayed here, he'd only get feebler, and that would compromise his chances of helping Elizabeth. At least on shore, he could find cover.

Maybe if he lowered himself into the water. But no... there were alligators. They could smell blood. He had to get off this boat, though, or Boss would find him and take advantage of his weakened state.

Too bad the rope ladder was on the other side of the boat.

He'd surely be caught if he tried to make it there. He looked around, surveying his options.

There. Just behind him was the rudder, and above it, a little step, probably built for repair access. He could sit on it. It wasn't ideal, but it would hide him a little better until he figured out what to do next.

Inside he heard more talking. A sly look in the window confirmed that all three were in the cabin. Shorty sat on the same barrel Evan had used, holding another gun and rubbing his sore head. How many guns did they have? Elizabeth was bound and gagged, and a fresh wave of angry determination flooded Evan's spirit. If only he could get a clear shot, but Boss had placed himself at an angle, so Elizabeth blocked him from the window and Shorty blocked him from the door. And since Boss still had the gun trained on Elizabeth, even a shot at Shorty was too risky.

Especially since the gun he'd taken from the man was an Allen & Thurber Single Shot. If Evan was going to shoot, he'd better not miss.

As covertly as possible, he slunk to the anchor rope and slid down, balancing himself on the small wooden ledge. Ever so carefully, he positioned himself where he was seated on the ledge, with his legs dangling over the rudder. From here, maybe he could get to shore without being seen. But he didn't dare risk it yet. He was too weak. He felt for the knife in his opposite boot, strapped to his calf. Still there. He loosened it and clung to the ivory handle. This and the single shot were his only weapons against outlaws and predators. He couldn't afford to lose either of them beneath the waters.

He wondered how Amelia was doing. One of the most capable women he'd ever met, she'd certainly do her best to assist in Elizabeth's rescue. But Amelia was a writer, not a Ranger, and she was out of her element here.

Just in case, Evan knew he needed to figure out this rescue as if he were the only one available. *God, I've said this so many times in the last twenty-four hours. I don't know what I'm doing. I guess Amelia's not the only one who's out of her element. Please, get us all out of this alive.* He waited for what seemed a very long time.

Waited and prayed and tried to ignore the throbbing that taunted him with every breath.

He'd been at some pretty low places in his lifetime. But so far, his worst difficulties had affected him more than others, and he'd had to work through them for his own sake. This time, he was faced with a hero's challenge. Succeed, and the women he loved would be safe. Fail, and...

Failure simply wasn't an option.

~

*G*od must have heard her prayers, because it wasn't long until Amelia saw a small boat headed her way, carrying Brody and Sheriff Goodman. She reined in Abby and waved her arms over her head. The shock on the sheriff's face was worth a thousand front page stories, and Amelia tucked the memory away so she could write about it later. He started to call out, but she held her finger to her lips.

The water carried sound, and the last thing she needed was for Boss or Shorty to get wind of their discussion. The sheriff caught her message and steered the boat toward shore. Within minutes, he climbed into the soggy marsh and waded to her and Abby.

"Fancy seein' you here. Where's Elizabeth? Have you seen Evan?"

Amelia nodded. "They're just around that bend. I escaped, but they're both on the boat with the two kidnappers, and each of them has a gun."

"Evan and Elizabeth both have a gun?" Goodman looked surprised.

"No. Shorty and Boss. Evan's pistol got soaked. Boss made him drop it in the water by threatening to shoot Elizabeth. I have his rifle. But come to think of it, Evan may have stolen Shorty's gun..." Amelia tried to make sense of all she'd seen and heard from shore.

While they spoke, Brody tied the boat to a strong limb, then joined them. "So we have two armed men and two captives?"

"Evan is hiding on the boat. At least, he was when I left. Boss and Shorty have Elizabeth."

Goodman removed his hat and scratched his head. "Evan was supposed to make them believe he was Rett. And he was supposed to wait until we arrived."

Amelia explained, in as much detail as she could, all that had transpired. Her brain felt like a rattled mess, but somehow it helped her nerves to pour out the story. It would have been better to spill it onto the page in hand-written therapy, but for now, talking would have to do.

While she spoke, Goodman and Brody just listened, nodded here and there, and occasionally looked at one another. Finally she took a deep breath and realized she'd been clipping words like a racehorse clipped dust. She hoped she'd made sense, because now she didn't want to repeat herself.

Neither man responded for a moment, as if waiting to make sure she had nothing more to add. Goodman turned to his deputy, eyed him up and down and said, "You'll have to be Rett."

Of course. Brody would work as a stand-in for Ranger Smith. Not perfect. Brody was several inches shorter and dark-haired. But it was either Brody or Goodman, and considering the older man's paunch and bald head, she doubted Boss would believe it. Why, even Shorty wouldn't buy it.

"How much time do we have?" Goodman looked at his pocket watch as he asked the question.

"He's giving Evan five hours to bring Rett to him. But it took

138

me at least an hour to find you two, maybe more. We don't have much time."

The sheriff nodded. "We'll leave the boat here. Take us through the woods and show us where they are."

The sun was already beginning its descent on the horizon as Amelia led the two men to a secluded spot where they could view the boat without being detected. Evan was no longer on the boat's portside. Where was he?

Oh, my. There, perched on a tiny ledge above the rudder, was Evan.

～

*N*early an hour passed, though it seemed like longer as Evan waited for some swamp critter to show up. Twice, he'd almost slid into the water in an attempt to swim to shore, but his leg was in worse shape than he'd realized. He couldn't use it to propel himself forward, and he thought the effort it would take to stroke, and to kick with his other leg, would be more than he could bear. He was afraid he'd get halfway to shore and go under, or be attacked by a hungry reptile.

Besides, every quarter hour or so, Shorty came out of the cabin, circled the deck with a rifle, and went back inside. So far, Evan had managed to press against the boat each time he heard footsteps, and avoid being seen. If Evan was going to make it to shore, he had to go right after Shorty went inside, or he'd run out of time before he got there.

After a while, he caught some movement from the bank. Amelia. Along with Goodman and Brody. Oh, thank God. Help had arrived.

He had no idea what was happening on deck, but at least he felt pretty certain Elizabeth wouldn't be harmed for a couple more hours. At least, that's what he hoped. But time was ticking away. *God, keep us safe.*

He squinted through the twilight. Amelia was signing again.

"B-r-o-d-y w-i-l-l p-r-e-t-e-n-d t-o b-e R-e-t-t." Evan nodded.

"C-a-n y-o-u s-w-i-m t-o s-h-o-r-e?"

Evan shook his head, then signed, "M-y l-e-g h-u-r-t-s t-o-o b-a-d-l-y."

She didn't look happy. Even through the dim light, he could see the set of her mouth, could read the unspoken thoughts. *I told you so.*

Well, badge or no badge, he would have come after them. He wouldn't have had a choice even if he hadn't been a Ranger. What did she expect him to do, sit in his office and twiddle his thumbs while a couple of brutes did who-knew-what to the two most important people in his life?

Surely she couldn't still be holding his Ranger status against him, could she?

Yeah. She could. That was one stubborn little woman.

He felt so helpless, sitting on that tiny ledge in the middle of this backwater bayou, watching Amelia and the sheriff and Brody make plans on shore. After a few minutes, the two men retreated into the woods, leaving Amelia standing, watching him from the shadows. He didn't like that they'd left her alone, but she was holding the rifle. They must have felt she was safer there.

He supposed for the time being, he'd have to be content to wait and pray.

～

*A*melia had noticed something on her journey back through the woods. It was well-hidden, to be sure. But not so well-hidden that the bow didn't stick out from beneath the pile of leaves, along with an oar handle. It looked more like someone had hidden it there, not like it had been there a long time. As soon as Brody and Goodman were out of sight, she backtracked to the spot and brushed the dead leaves aside.

Just as she'd thought. A canoe.

The sheriff had told her to watch and wait. Had said they were going to scope things out first. Then they'd be back. But she couldn't wait. Wouldn't wait.

It was getting dark. Evan needed medical attention, and he needed to be rescued from... She didn't even want to think of all the possible villains that could cause him harm at this moment. Surely she could row out there and get him. She and the two men had watched for a time before they got Evan's attention. Shorty came out every quarter hour to walk around deck and check on things. If she stayed quiet and timed it right after he returned to the cabin, it wouldn't be hard. She hoped.

Boss wouldn't expect them to return with Rett for at least two or three more hours, and what did Evan plan to do? Perch there like a pigeon all through Elizabeth's rescue?

No. There was no choice. He needed rescuing too, and God had provided a canoe. She'd quietly row out there and bring him back to shore. She was no nurse, but at least she could get the man she loved out of harm's way, perhaps bandage his wound while they waited.

Uh...she meant Evan. Not the man she loved. Not anymore.

With a great heave, she tugged on the boat and landed square on her backside. The canoe moved a couple of feet, maybe.

Well, if it had to be moved one foot at a time, so be it.

In reality, it was more inch-by-inch. Boy, she never realized how little strength she had in her arms. Maybe if she pushed instead of pulled.

No, that was just as hard.

She stood up and tried to figure out a better way. Finally,

she sat down and used her legs to push. There. The boat moved forward a good three feet. She scooted forward again, and push. Scoot, push. Scoot, push until the bow touched the water's edge. She gave it one more push, a gentle one this time, and grabbed the stern to keep the canoe from gliding out too far.

She sat down in the boat, placed the rifle across her knees and felt around for the oar. Who was the hero now? Ha. And she didn't need to wear a badge to prove it. All was quiet. The kerosene light flickered in the dusk through the cabin's window, and she could barely see Evan still clinging to the rope. This should be easy enough.

Using the oar to push off from shore, she slid silently through the inky waters, feeling quite pleased with herself.

Something in front of her caught her attention. What was that?

She was sure something had moved. *Oh, molasses.*

A snake was right there, not two feet from her.

He looked right at her, almost seemed to sigh in sinful antic-ipation, and in that slithery smile she saw what looked like white lips. Did snakes have lips? Well, this one looked to. Another hiss revealed the serpent was actually opening his mouth, and the white she saw came from the inside lining of his jaw.

A cottonmouth. One of the deadliest snakes in the world.

Or at least in these parts.

What happened next was more reaction than reason, as she picked up her paddle and whacked the thing. Then, using the blade of the paddle, she pinned the snake to the bottom of the boat, pressing harder and harder until she felt a crunch, and knew she'd crushed its spine. Only, it was still writhing. *Oh, God, oh God, oh God. Are You there? Help.*

Using the paddle now as a scoop, she gathered up the offending beast and slung it into the water, away from Evan and as far away from the boat as she could fling it. Which wasn't far enough for her.

~

*E*van could feel himself grow weaker by the minute. If he could only rest, that would be different. But as it was, he had to use all his strength to hold on to the tiny wooden ledge so he didn't fall off.

He heard shuffling on shore. What was Amelia doing? He closed his eyes for a moment and willed her to stay put. Some days, that girl didn't have the common sense of a gnat. Particularly when she got an idea in her head. It was as if she had blinders on and could see nothing but what she chose to see.

But then he opened his eyes, saw what she was doing and felt a moment of guilt for mentally berating her. She was coming to get him. The tables had turned, and now she was the rescuer. He sucked in a breath, in bated expectation of finally being on dry land, finally being able to examine his wound properly, finally being able see the boat and cabin that held his sister more clearly. On shore, he'd be able to make plans, shoot the rifle, do something besides perch uselessly on a ledge.

How long had it been since Shorty made his rounds?

Only a few minutes. Maybe there was time...

Wait. Something was wrong, He could see it in her face. She—

No. He watched her lift up from her seat, aim the paddle toward the front end of the boat, and bam! She whacked some poor soul with all her might.

Fortunately, the whack didn't make too much of a sound. What in the world was in that boat with her, that made her hold that paddle against the bow and push with all her might?

He didn't have to wait long to find out. After a moment, she flung the remains of a snake into the water. Alligators and snakes. If they ever got out of this thing alive, perhaps they should all pack up and move back to Boston...

She held out the paddle to him, and he grabbed it, pulling her and the canoe as close to the boat as he could. She looked like she'd burst into tears any second, but to her credit she remained silent.

"Who's there?" Shorty shouted from above them, and Evan put his finger over his mouth as he held Amelia's eyes. After a time, Shorty's footsteps retreated back into the cabin.

"That was quite the show," he finally whispered.

"A cottonmouth was in the boat. What was I supposed to do?" Irritation seeped through Amelia's voice.

"It's all right. You did well. I'm proud of you." He looked at the remains of the snake, floating toward them now.

"It's still moving." Her whispered voice bordered on hysteria, and though he felt the same way, he had to keep calm for her sake. A cottonmouth could be dangerous even if it was dead. The venom from just one bite might not kill, but it could incapacitate a person enough to drown. Plus, where there was one cottonmouth, there were usually several, as they built nests. And multiple bites would most definitely kill a person.

They had to get out of here.

CHAPTER 18

*A*melia felt paralyzed.. All around her were snakes in the water. And alligators. And who knew what else. Above her, in the boat, two armed men held Elizabeth prisoner. Was there no safe place?

She was glad Evan had the wherewithal to take over from that point, because she'd stretched her fortitude about as far as it would go. Silently he climbed down from his roost and settled himself on the opposite seat. He took the paddle and, without a word, began rowing back to shore.

Somewhere in her mind, she knew she should be doing the rowing. After all, Evan was injured. But she didn't protest, and in a short time they were in the massive root system and couldn't row any farther.

With a great heave of relief, she grabbed the rifle with one hand and reached out to Evan with the other, offering what little support she could. Together they abandoned the canoe and sloshed the rest of the way to shore. They'd made it. Mostly in one piece.

Good thing dusk hadn't yet given way to dark, or they'd have been feeling through the roots and crevices. Instead, they gingerly found their way to dry land, and Evan lowered himself to the ground in what looked to be a mixture of discomfort and momentary consolation.

Amelia dropped to her knees beside him and tried to think of something soothing to say when another noise— this time coming from dry land—nearly sent her to her grave for perhaps the fourth time that day.

"What are you trying to do, Missy? Get yourself assassinated?"

It was Goodman, whispering—no, more like hissing at her. And she'd been hissed at enough for one day.

∽

*E*van closed his eyes and tried to shut out the hushed argument taking place above him, tried to shut out the intense throbbing that shot up his leg, through his spine, and into his shoulders. He felt weak. Weaker than he'd realized.

"He's hurt," Amelia snapped. "I couldn't just leave him out there, and I didn't know how long it would be."

"I could see you standing up in the canoe with the paddle."

Silence.

"I said, tell me what happened out there." More silence.

"Amelia. Tell me what happened, young lady."

Big mistake, Evan thought to himself. If Sheriff Goodman wanted to get anywhere with Amelia, he was going about it all wrong. "There was a snake in the boat." Evan spoke, but his tongue felt thick and dry despite his sopping state. "Cottonmouth."

"Shh, Evan. You rest. I'll handle the sheriff." Amelia's voice was like a silky balm, caressing his spirit. She sounded like she cared. Was it possible she'd changed her mind about him? But just as quickly, her voice turned to kerosene again. "See what you did? He's not in any shape to talk. Yes, there was a big, fat cottonmouth in my boat. He must have crawled in from the water, because he sure wasn't there when I got in. He was ten feet long and coming after me."

"Ten feet?" Brody sounded skeptical.

"More like four," Evan croaked, though he immediately wanted to take it back. Best not to contradict a woman on the edge of hysteria.

Goodman grunted something, but Evan couldn't understand what. Amelia held his hand. She stroked his head, and he could practically feel the tension in her fingers. She was mad. And worried about him. And scared half witless.

Soon, he felt his leg being jostled, and he bit back a moan. Man, that hurt. He opened his eyes, and Goodman was rummaging through his pack.

A ripping sound...somebody was cutting away his pant leg. He wondered if they were using his knife. No, he felt it in his other boot, where he'd replaced it during his long wait on the little ledge.

Something cold and hot and fiery hit the wound, and this time he did moan. What was that?

"It's just some alcohol, Evan. It'll stop the infection, if there is any. I'm gonna let that work on you for a few minutes. Then I'll wrap it." To Amelia, Goodman said, "We've gotta figure out something to use for bandages."

"We can use my petticoat," she offered.

"That would work great if it were dry. If you'll hang it from one of these trees overnight, it might be dry by morning. We'll need to change the bandages then. But for now, look in his pack and see what you can find."

He heard Amelia walk away, wanted to call for her, but he didn't have the strength. He'd thought he was doing fine until they got to shore. But when he collapsed, he was done, at least for the time being.

"It's wet, but that's okay. Salt water's good for a wound. Slows the bleeding and any infection. I'm gonna rub some honey on this before I wrap it. I always carry some with me. My grandma taught me it was good for healing wounds. Tastes great on a biscuit, too." Goodman was talking while he fumbled through his supplies, though Evan wasn't sure to whom. Himself, maybe? Or perhaps he spoke for Evan's benefit. Honey. Interesting...he'd heard of the Indians or the pioneers or somebody putting honey on wounds... He reminded himself to look into that later...

Evan must have lost consciousness then, because the next thing he knew, they were lifting his head and placing something soft beneath it.

"All done," Amelia said. "Sorry about your white dress shirt. I found it in your saddlebag. At least I know you have others."

~

*A*melia wanted to wake up and realize this was all some zany nightmare, starting with just after lunch yesterday. Or was that day before yesterday? She'd lost track.

She watched Evan sleep, embracing him with her eyes.

Oh, Evan. Why did you have to go and become a Ranger?

It wasn't as if he had something to prove. He was her hero, fighting injustice with knowledge instead of a gun. She had her writing, and he had the courtroom. They would have made a great team.

But not anymore. He could tell her a thousand times that he'd give the badge back after the Rangers returned from their assignment, but she'd never believe him. Not now. Once a lawman, always a lawman. That's what Gerald used to say. And look where that got him.

Amelia was sure it was no different with a Ranger's badge than a US marshal's badge. And she wouldn't have any part of it.

No, they'd get through this together. But once this night-

148

mare was over, she'd move on. Mr. Thomas had plenty of connections. Perhaps he could set her up somewhere far away. Somewhere where she'd never run into Evan.

A hint of a burning wood smell caused her to look from the object of her attention, and she realized the sheriff and Brody had started a small campfire behind several of the larger tree trunks, about fifty feet back. Not visible from Boss's boat. She hoped.

Would they smell it on the boat? No. The breeze was moving off the water, not toward it. Ideally, they'd be okay. She hated that Evan was here, not thirty feet from the water's edge, but he'd gotten this far and collapsed. At least he was in the shadows. And it was a good spot to view the boat without being seen. *Thank you, God, for the moon lighting the boat. I appreciate it tonight more than ever.*

She stood then, wrapping her arms around herself, and realized she was shivering. She really should go and dry herself out. As if he could read her thoughts, Sheriff Goodman approached. "Go warm up by the fire. I'll sit with him a while. In a few minutes, I'll come talk to you about the plans."

Amelia nodded and obeyed. The fire did beckon her. Besides its drying powers, the smoke would surely keep the mosquitoes at bay.

Brody sat by the fire cleaning a pistol of some sort. She thought of Evan's pistol, which he'd dropped in the water near the alligator. He was sure to want that back. Where had she— oh, yes. It was in his pack, safe with Abby. Maybe Brody would clean it, too, to keep it from ruining. Without a word, she retrieved the pistol and handed it to the young deputy. He took it, turned it over a couple of times, and seemed to need no explanation. Just set his own gun aside and began cleaning that one.

For the first time in a couple of hours, at least, Amelia let her mind wander to Elizabeth. Was she okay? Was she frightened? Did she think Amelia had abandoned her?

A crushing feeling rose in Amelia's chest then. Here she was, safely on shore. Those men weren't after Amelia. But the danger to Elizabeth's life was real. *God, I don't want to lose Elizabeth. She's my friend. We're the same, a couple of misfits in a man's world. Please don't take her.*

She thought of Evan, and her chest clenched even more. Elizabeth was all Evan had left. If anything happened to her... he'd be truly alone. And though she refused to consider him a suitable partner for marriage, she didn't hate him.

Truth was, she loved him. And the thought of him bearing the weight of the loss of his only living relative, the thought of the intense loneliness that would surely follow... Before she knew it, she was on her knees beside the log, sobbing out loud but praying in her heart. *Please, God. Please don't take her. Don't do that to Evan.*

A gentle hand rested on her shoulder, but she pushed it away. "Miss Cooper, it's alright. Don't cry, Miss Cooper."

Poor Brody. She'd seen it before—most single men felt help-less in the presence of a sobbing woman. But she just didn't have it in her to cork the tears for his sake. No, these tears needed to be shed. What was that she'd read? Something about how God heard our prayers and saw our tears. That he would answer. *Well, here I am, God. Do you see me? Do you hear me? Please. Please make this stop. Please protect Evan and Elizabeth. They need each other.*

"Miss Cooper." Sheriff Goodman stood beside her. What did he want? The big bully. She was still mad at him. "I know you've been through an ordeal, but I need you to calm down. It's nine o'clock. Brody will need to go out there soon. If you want to help Evan and Elizabeth, you need to tell me everything you know about the men who kidnapped you. Start from the beginning."

Help them? All right. She took some deep breaths to calm herself. This was so unlike her. She needed something to—oh. There. Sheriff Goodman held out his handkerchief for her, and she blew her nose in the most indelicate fashion. Then she wiped her tears on her sleeve, sat up tall, and proceeded to tell the entire story, from the beginning. She was almost to the part where she taught Elizabeth to sign the alphabet when the still night was interrupted by a scream.

Elizabeth.

CHAPTER 19

*E*van was jolted from oblivion at the sound of his sister's scream. What was happening? What time was it? After eight, surely. He felt around for the rifle, but it wasn't there. Where was the sheriff? Where was Amelia?

He tried to stand up, but his head swirled. Or the trees swirled around him. He wasn't sure which, but regardless, he figured standing wasn't such a good idea at the moment.

Then, through the gathering darkness, he heard Boss bellowing and some scuffling.

"You unruly little scamp. What have you done?"

Elizabeth screamed again, and Evan strained to peer into the dark. He could see a faint light through the dusk. One of them was holding a lantern.

The moon allowed a brief moment of illumination before clouds moved to hide it, and Evan saw his sister. That goon was holding her by her hair. Why, that—

Amelia, Goodman, and Brody joined Evan then on the bank. Boss bellowed some more, and the tension among the four on shore as they watched in silent disbelief was weighty and thick.

More yelling. "I refuse to stand by and let you kill my

husband, or my brother. You're going to kill me anyway. Do it now, you coward."

Oh, Elizabeth.

The sheriff and Brody drew their guns, but there was no chance for a clear shot. Elizabeth was too close. After a moment, the sheriff whispered to Evan. "We need to expedite our plans. Call out to him. Let him know you're here and that you have Rett."

Whereas a moment before Evan had felt shaky and feeble, he now felt a superhuman empowerment he knew came from a Source beyond himself. He inhaled a broad gulp of air and called forth a stalwart sound he hoped was convincing. "Let go of her right now. I've got her husband here."

Elizabeth gasped. "Rett?"

Brody didn't miss a beat. "I'm here, sweetheart. I'm coming out."

Just a sliver of a pause. Then she called, "Okay, honey." But that pause was enough to alert Boss of their scheme.

He wasn't fooled. "That ain't yer husband. If it had been, you'd have told him to stay put, 'cause you don't want him to get killed. Who ya got out there, Covington? A whole bevy of gunslingers, no doubt, with their guns all pointed directly at me. Well, guess what? You shoot me, you shoot yer sister."

More scuffle, and Evan knew Elizabeth was fighting Boss. Where was the other guy? Shorty?

Goodman spoke next to Evan's ear. "We're gonna have to sneak around in the brush to get a better shot. See if you can keep him talking." The sheriff and Brody murmured to each other for a moment, then headed in opposite directions. It looked like they were going to aim at the boat from both sides.

"Nobody out here wants anyone to get shot. We just want Elizabeth to be safe. Let her go, and I'll make sure you don't hang." Evan worked to keep his voice strong.

"What? And spend the rest of my life in the stockade? No,

thanks. I know I'll die tonight. But I plan to enjoy the sweet taste of revenge first."

"What if I let you go? I'll make sure you have a head start. I'm wounded, and Elizabeth needs medical attention. I'll stall, give you time to get away before allowing anyone to come after you."

"You lie, and we both know it. Those woods are crawling with lawmen. I can smell 'em. I think we need to end this thing right now."

More scuffle. Then a gun went off, followed by a second shot. Someone yelped, but Evan couldn't tell who. *Oh, dear God, no. Please, no.* Evan tried again to stand, but Amelia held him.

"No. I won't let you go out there. It would be suicide." Amelia's voice cracked as she spoke.

"Let go of me. Elizabeth, are you all right?"

"I'm okay, Evan." More scuffle.

Thank you, God. Keep protecting her.

"She's alive," Boss roared. "But thanks to her, I've got a hurt foot and Lance is nearly dead. Bleeding to death, right in front of me. That makes two friends she's responsible for killing."

Another bullet whizzed through the night—this time it came from Evan's left—and pinged off the metal boat railing. Brody?

Evan didn't know when he'd felt so helpless. *God, we need more light. How can I protect Elizabeth if I can't see?*

That's when an unexplainable, unreasonable calm enveloped his conscience, and he felt as if God were speaking to his spirit —*Trust me.*

"Evan." Elizabeth's voice confirmed once again that she was alive.

Of course I trust you, Lord. But Elizabeth's out there.

And there it was again. *Trust me.*

Well, under the circumstances, Evan didn't have much choice. He couldn't see very well. He could barely move. Trust God? He would have to.

"If you can make it to the canoe, perhaps we can paddle out

to her." A sliver of moonlight caught Amelia's Rembrandt features as she whispered, and the pang in Evan's soul intensified again. He'd lost her, and he was about to lose Elizabeth, too.

"They'd kill us before we got there. But maybe we can take cover behind one of the trees. I'm a pretty good shot..."

"That doesn't surprise me."

Evan took a deep breath. He had to keep going through the pain. "I'll need you to help me."

Together, with him leaning on her tiny frame, they maneuvered to the water's edge, where moonbeams tickled the slumbering waves. Under different circumstances, it might have been romantic. "We need to move closer and to the right. I think I can get a clear shot." Evan kept his eyes on Elizabeth.

"If we go there, we won't have anything to shield us. It's too risky."

"You're right. You stay behind this tree, and I'll move over there and try to get a clear aim."

Amelia huffed. "I'm not letting you do that."

Evan didn't have the energy to fight with her. Together they moved through the marshy roots, staying as low to the surface as they could without getting the gun wet.

                          ~

A boom sounded from somewhere behind them, and Amelia felt her whole body clench in fear. If Brody and the sheriff weren't careful, they'd shoot Elizabeth.

"That the best you've got?" Boss bellowed. "You cowards. Step out from behind those trees. Come out here and fight like men."

This he yelled while using Elizabeth as a shield, gun pointed at her chest. Who was he calling cowardly?

Clouds parted, and the moon illuminated the area. Then, as

they watched, Boss pulled back the hammer. Pressed his finger to the trigger. Time froze. Amelia held her breath.

Watched Elizabeth buck the man, bite down on his arm.

Watched him drop the gun as it fired.

Watched Boss reach for her, hit her with the back of his hand.

She was vaguely aware of Evan steadying the gun, siting it on Boss. He held the firearm to his shoulder but was clearly too weak to keep it there on his own. In one fluid motion, Amelia moved behind him, reached around his chest, and helped him steady the weapon.

Together, they fired the shot that hit Boss's shoulder and sent him backward into the wall of the boat's cabin, and sank him to the deck.

Elizabeth let out a brief scream, then stood there, hands to her mouth, staring at the man who had tried to take her life. After a moment she moved forward and picked up Boss's gun, which he'd dropped on deck.

Evan lowered the rifle, letting the barrel sink below the water in the marshy roots. At that point, it didn't really seem to matter if it got wet or not.

～

He'd done it. Evan had shot Boss and saved his sister from death.

Well, he and Amelia had done it together. With a little help from God.

"Good shot, boy." Sheriff Goodman appeared from the brush. "And you, little lady. I'm impressed. You've got some starch." He waded out and patted them each on the back. "Now we've gotta get that boat in. Amelia, you think you can take care of the Ranger here while Brody and I see to Elizabeth?"

"Yes." Amelia's voice was husky, and Evan could tell she was trying not to cry. Again. In the last few hours, he'd witnessed a whole new side to Amelia. Two new sides, really. The rugged side, and the hysterical side. Thus far in their relationship, she'd been pretty rock-steady, only showing extreme emotion when she was excited about a story.

Brody swam to the boat, while Goodman waded only up to his chest. Amelia and Evan sat in silence for a while, watching. After a time, Amelia stood and held out her hand to him.

"Up you go. It's over. Time you started acting like an invalid, at least until we get that leg healed."

"Amelia, I—"

"Come on. Up."

He got the message. She didn't want to converse. Didn't want to ruin this moment of triumph with the sadness of their failed attempt at courtship. He wanted to talk and drill some sense into her, but considering he'd been shot and wounded just as she'd predicted, he really didn't have a leg to stand on. Literally.

So instead, he tried to memorize the feel of her arm around his waist as she helped him hobble back to his resting spot, tried to etch the memory of her gentle hands on his wounded leg as she propped it on a log.

She dropped to the ground beside him, and together they watched as Brody lifted the anchor, then tossed a rope to Sheriff Goodman. The older man wound the rope between his thumb and elbow, then turned and, step by labored step, pulled the boat toward shore.

All this time, Elizabeth sat at the railing, her legs dangling over the edge of the boat, head leaned against the iron rail. She held Boss's gun pointed at the fallen captor.

Finally, when the boat was close enough to tie to a tree, Amelia stood. "I'd better go check on her."

Evan nodded, but hated to see her go. He didn't know if she'd ever be that close to him again. He propped his head against the tree and touched the place on his arm where her hand had last rested. Remaining in that position, he watched as one woman he loved climbed the rope ladder to the other woman he loved. Watched them embrace and crumple into tears in that way women did, that way that was entirely appropriate for them, given the circumstances.

His emotions, on the other hand, would have to wait until he was without an audience.

CHAPTER 20

*A*melia couldn't help feeling discombobulated after all was said and done. It was almost as if her emotions had temporarily fled, leaving a mechanical body behind to perform the remaining duties of the day. She helped shoot a man. Saw that Evan was as comfortable as possible, considering he was wet and wounded. Waded out to check on Elizabeth, whom she found in a sobbing mess on deck. It wasn't until she offered her friend a perfunctory hug that her senses returned, and the two shared in the appropriate sobs and sniffles of relief and disbelief.

"Did this really"—sob!—"ha-a-a-a-appen?" Elizabeth's words were difficult to understand through the blubbering, but somehow, Amelia was able to translate. In the past couple of days, she'd learned to speak hysteria too.

"Unfortunately, yes. But it's over now. You're safe. I'm safe. Evan and Rett are safe. It's all good."

The two sat side by side while Brody and Sheriff Goodman handcuffed Boss. She heard a muffled groan behind her, and for the first time, Amelia thought of the other man on board.

As if reading her mind, Elizabeth spoke again, this time a bit more clearly. "Shorty...he took a bullet for me. Pulled Boss's arm down and away. I can't believe it."

Amelia left Elizabeth at the railing and knelt beside the bleeding man. "Lance. Lance, can you hear me?"

He opened his eyes.

"That was a noble thing you did, protecting Elizabeth that way. I knew you weren't like Boss."

Shorty gave a slight nod, then winced from the pain it seemed to cause.

"Lance, I promised you money. I'm so sorry, Lance. I was trying to figure out a way to escape. I don't have any money. At least not nearly the amount I told you. I'm sorry I lied." He sucked in a deep breath, focused his eyes on hers, and with laborsome effort, replied, "I—didn't—do it for—the money." Then he drew his final breath, and Amelia wept again until her soul felt parched and cracked.

Brody called to them, then stood at the top of the rope ladder and assisted the two ladies down, while Goodman reached for them from the bottom. As soon as Elizabeth was free of the boat, she sloshed as quickly as she could through the bog to her hero-brother. Amelia kept her distance, allowing them their privacy.

Thank You, God, for answering my prayers. Evan won't be alone. He has his sister.

And then, odd as it was at the moment, a pang of jealousy stabbed through the cracks of her dry spirit. Most women would be glad to marry a hero like Evan. Surely he wouldn't always be a bachelor

~

*I*t was a long night. Even with the moonlight, it was too dark to make their way through the cypress and marsh, back to town. Evan felt pretty useless with his wound, but Elizabeth helped in that respect by clinging to his arm and staggering between joyous relief and frenzied recollections of the last day. Evan might not be able to help set up camp, but at least his presence offered a bit of comfort for his sister.

He watched as Amelia and Brody retrieved whatever useful goods they could find on the boat. She once again proved her mettle as they prepared a campsite in a dry spot in the woods. Boss bellowed insults at her a couple of times but closed his trap after Goodman threatened to lead him to a nest of cotton-mouths he'd stumbled upon earlier. Evan reminded himself to ask the sheriff, later, if the man really knew where such a nest was located.

Back was Amelia's determined efficiency. She bustled and scurried and cared for Elizabeth, and even brought Evan a cup of coffee fresh from the fire and sat with him a for a brief time, just to make sure he was comfortable. But other than those few awkward minutes, she kept her distance.

The journey back to Goose Creek the next morning was interesting, to say the least. After several failed attempts to transport both Shorty's body and Boss—incapacitated but not mortally wounded—to the local jail, they gave up, covered Shorty as reverently as possible, and vowed to return for him later. Evan got the feeling if it weren't for the women, Goodman would have tossed the deceased ruffian to the alligators.

Once in town, it didn't take long for Norma Rae to find them and insist they take lunch at her restaurant. "On the house," she said, and the smile she wore made her lined face wrinkle like an apple from last year's supply. She treated Evan like the King of England, pulling a special chair from the back, propping him with pillows, covering him with a hand-made quilt and calling him a hero, insisting the sheriff set up a parade for him once they returned to Houston.

But Evan didn't care much for all the foofaraw. He would have traded every bit of it for a single glance from Amelia, who had done a fine job of avoiding him for the last twelve hours. But Norma Rae—that woman didn't miss a thing. She must have seen Evan watching Amelia, and the older woman made a big fuss over insisting Amelia sit next to Evan and help feed him.

"It's my leg that's shot, Norma Rae," Evan told the woman. "There's nothing wrong with my arms."

"Now you just hush," she said. "Young lady—what was your name again? Azalea?—I can't be in the kitchen and out here at the same time. I need you to help me take care of this feller."

Amelia started to protest, but then appeared to see the futility of the situation and pulled up a chair next to Evan. After an awkward moment, Evan spoke first. "So...Azalea. How are you this morning?"

That brought a smile. "I've been better. But all things considered, not bad."

An awkward silence settled between them, despite the chatter around them as Sheriff Goodman, Brody and Elizabeth answered questions from a few locals. Boss sulked from his place between Goodman and Brody but said nothing. The man had been shot twice. Once in the little toe, by Shorty. The second time, he was shot in the shoulder. Now, wounds wrapped, it was hard to tell what caused the wretched man more grief—the bullet holes, the gaping hole in his pride or his failed attempt at revenge.

"What's a matter there, fella? You got a bo-bo on your toe-toe?" The sheriff was relentless with his prisoner, and under different circumstances Evan might have felt sorry for the man. Instead, he just chuckled under his breath and thanked God things had turned out as they did.

At least all the hullabaloo kept him from having to make much small talk with Amelia. He scanned his mind for something to say, something that wouldn't be considered pushy.

Something easy and noncontroversial. "This will make some story. You'll get the front page, for sure."

"True," Amelia answered, rubbing her finger around the rim of her coffee mug. "But I'm not interested in being on the front page, unless my name is on the byline."

"Surely Mr. Thomas will let you write your own story for this." Evan had no doubt this would give her an even bigger career boost than his own story had.

"I hope so. He may give me the excuse that I can't write it because I'm not an unbiased source, or some other rubbish."

Evan nodded. They'd covered her writing. What else could they talk about that wouldn't be too painful?

She looked as miserable as he felt. After another uncomfortable lull between them, she opened her mouth like she was going to say something, but they were saved from further embarrassment, at least for the moment. Norma Rae chose that instant to bluster out of the kitchen and plop down a heaping basket of hot, buttery rolls.

His mouth watered just looking at them. Then Norma Rae refilled his coffee cup, as well as everyone else's, and began taking their breakfast orders.

At least that bought them a few more minutes. Boy. The pain in his heart was so much worse than the pain in his leg.

$\sim$

*I*t took all of Amelia's will and then some not to look at, stare at, savor every one of Evan's handsome features. He looked good. He looked so good, despite the fact he hadn't shaved or used soap in two days, despite the fact that his hair stuck to his head in a sweaty, curly mess, despite the fact that he still wore remnants of swamp muck.

So she tried—unsuccessfully—to distract herself by

spreading butter on a roll for him, lest Norma Rae scold her for not doing her job. That's when the conversation turned lethal.

"Hey, Covington," the sheriff said, then took a long swallow of coffee before he continued. When he had everyone's attention, he set down the mug. "For an educated city-slicker, you didn't do half-bad. I'm impressed."

Evan looked to be at a momentary loss for words. He nodded and offered that adorable half smile that showed off his dimple.

Amelia forced herself to examine the pattern on the faded tablecloth instead.

Goodman continued. "You plannin' on keepin' that Ranger badge?"

She sucked in a breath. The desire to look at him, lock her eyes on his beautiful green ones, pulled at her with centrifugal force. But she fought it, instead noting that one thread of the tablecloth, running through the entire length of the fabric, wasn't symmetrical with the others.

She felt Evan stiffen. Felt his eyes on her, though she refused to meet them. Felt the thickness of that long, painful pause before he cleared his throat and answered the question.

"I can't say I've enjoyed the last couple of days, but I did find immense satisfaction in them."

"You're a natural. I don't see why you can't keep that fancy-dancy law office of yours and be a Ranger too, if you've a mind to do both," Brody interjected.

Amelia realized she'd stuck her entire thumb through what had been a miniscule hole in her napkin. Now she'd have to offer to replace it.

Evan shifted in his seat, rested his arm on the back of Amelia's chair. "Thank you for the compliment. But I think I'll be retiring my Ranger badge as soon as the other Rangers return."

She could hear the strain in his voice. He really was a natural

—the sheriff was right. He was good and true and honorable. He was rugged and wild and capable. His intelligence more than made up for any lack in—she couldn't think of a single thing he was lacking.

No. This was wrong. If Evan wanted to be a Ranger, he should be a Ranger. The world would certainly be a safer, nobler place with someone like Evan upholding the law both in the courtroom and in the streets. But he was giving up the opportunity.

For her.

She never knew guilt could weigh so much.

"Are you sure?" Elizabeth piped in from her side of the table. "It's a rare combination, what with your knowledge of the law and the ability to track, shoot with precision and not get ruffled under pressure."

Et tu, Brut é ?

Elizabeth's eyes met Amelia's briefly before the other woman looked away.

"Thank you for your confidence in me, but no. Sometimes we have to make choices. There are...other things that are more important to me than wearing a badge and a gun." Evan spoke to the entire group, but Amelia knew his words were intended for her.

Norma Rae, of course, had to have her say. "What do you mean, retire your badge? You can't retire your badge. I was hopin' I could convince you to come to Goose Creek. Why, I told you we already don't see near enough lawmen in these parts. Now you're tellin' me there's gonna be one less? What could possibly be more important than protecting innocent lives?" The woman slammed the coffeepot down on the table, and hot coffee sloshed onto the tablecloth, mottling the thread Amelia studied so intently.

A shawl of dense reticence cloaked the group, perfect complement to the scarf of shameful self-reproach Amelia's conscience already wore. The bulky emotion encumbered her spirit until she couldn't breathe. *God, I can't do this. What if he dies, like Gerald? Please don't make me do this.*

And there, in the center of her being, she sensed God's spirit urging her to not be afraid, to have faith, to trust Him.

Would she listen, or push Him away out of fear?

"No." She delivered the word with more force than she realized. It was such a tiny word, to hold such power. She felt everyone there watching her, felt them lean forward in expectation.

Finally Evan spoke. "What?"

She dragged her eyes to him, in spite of the knowledge that once she looked at him, she'd be his. Hopelessly, forever his. Yet she'd rather be trapped in Evan's love than in her own fear. And suddenly, it was as if a haze lifted and she saw herself clearly for the first time. She'd let herself be ruled by fear, and in so doing had confined herself and clipped her own wings.

Well, no more.

"You will not turn in your badge. Not unless you want to. Don't do it for me."

She didn't care that they had an audience. Didn't care about anything anymore, except making things right with the man she loved more than life itself. Her voice dropped to a whisper. "Ranger or not, I'm in love with you."

A grin the size of Texas covered his handsome face. "So... you'll let me court you? No matter what?"

"If you'll still have me."

That's when the whole audience thing really got in the way, as the two sat staring at one another, love oozing out of every pore, and yet—

"Well don't just sit there, Ranger. Kiss her." Norma Rae picked up the coffeepot and stood, waiting. It didn't appear she had any intention of moving from that spot until he followed her orders.

EPILOGUE

THREE MONTHS LATER

*T*urned out, being the society page reporter had its perks after all. The local florist, seamstress and caterer, and a bevy of shop owners offered their services at greatly reduced rates. All wanted to have their hand—and thus, their name—in what turned out to be the wedding of the decade.

Even the weather craved its share of the spotlight and showed up with sunny skies, mild temperatures and just a hint of a breeze. The pews of Calvary Church had never been so crowded, as the upper echelon bumped elbows with humble dockworkers. Seemed everybody wanted to witness Houston's beloved journalist marry the once–notorious, criminal–look-alike–turned–Ranger.

Outside the church, makeshift tables bowed with the weight of Norma Rae's rolls and delicacies, as well as the five-tier cake the woman had insisted on donating. Amelia never would have guessed such an eccentric character could have such exquisite taste, but the cake was lovely.

The day came on the heels of some other good news. Unbeknownst to Amelia, Mr. Thomas sent her front-page story to some high-powered New York publisher, and they wanted her to write a book. Under a pseudonym, of course, because apparently no one would believe such a tale could be written by a woman. It didn't take her long to decide on a pen name— Cooper Covington.

But even a book contract didn't fill up her heart the way Evan did. Yes, God had given her a second chance at love, and she'd almost thrown it away. But, as is so often the case, when God offers abundant grace, He also requires abundant faith. From those who claim to be His, He demands a dangerous, rugged devotion. But with that kind of reckless faith come God's bountiful blessings. And this day was evidence of such.

Yes, walking down the aisle that day required every bit of faith Amelia could muster, but muster it she had. God loved her. Evan loved her. And she refused to expect anything other than God's best.

She'd finally learned what fear was. The expectation of something bad. It was the opposite of hope, and God was a God of hope.

"You are more beautiful than any bride I've ever seen," Elizabeth whispered as she adjusted Amelia's veil once more.

The veil, along with the dress, was custom-made by the seamstress who'd taught Amelia sign language. The dress was cream silk with a high V-neck and gathered lace at each shoulder. Both dress and matching lace veil were embroidered at the hem with a border of tiny five-point stars, each framed in a circle of delicate rosebuds, forming, for the attentive observer, a series of Texas Ranger badges. Hanging delicately at the bride's neck was the opal necklace left behind on that fateful night, the perfect complement to the ring on her finger.

"I agree," Amelia's mother said, brushing back glistening

moisture before placing a kiss on her daughter's cheek. "I'd better find my seat."

"Yes, it's time," Amelia's father said, and she noticed his eyes were a bit shinier than usual.

Organ music sounded, and Elizabeth adjusted one more of Amelia's curls, then straightened the heirloom comb in her own hair before heading into the sanctuary.

When Amelia and her father stepped through the door, she was overcome. There was Mr. Thomas, looking more pleased than she'd ever seen him look. And there was Mrs. Lewison, the Widow Franklin and so many others she'd done stories on during the last couple of years. Why, everyone was there, standing from their seats and turning to see, beaming and grinning as if she were the first lady or something. And today, she was the first lady of Evan's heart, and that was more than enough to satisfy her.

There he was. Oh, he looked so handsome in his best suit and bow tie. But her favorite part of his attire covered his feet— a pair of alligator boots for which Amelia had paid a pretty penny. Every last bit of her savings had gone toward them and, though not from *the* alligator, they were special nonetheless.

Lined up next to him were Rett, Cody, and Ray, hair slicked into place, badges shining. They looked handsome, too, she supposed, though in her opinion, they paled in comparison with the groom.

Locking eyes with Evan, she inhaled and gripped her father's arm with one hand and her bouquet—pink rosebuds mixed with white stephanotis—with the other. The bouquet was gathered in a heavy silk ribbon, which trailed her skirt. But the best part, in her opinion, was what she'd focus on when she wrote about this for the society page. Pinned to the handle, at the top of one of the streaming ribbons, was Evan's Ranger badge.

The music faded out. She had a vague awareness of her father's sweet kiss on her cheek, and then he stepped from sight.

Everything turned to a haze around her, except for that one point of clarity from which she couldn't seem to withdraw her attention.

Evan's smiling face. The shine in his eyes.

The sound of his voice as he whispered, "You are more than I could have ever hoped for. I love you."

And the feeling of God smiling at her, as she pledged her love to the man who was her friend, her encourager and her hero.

Did you enjoy this book? We hope so!
Would you take a quick minute to leave a review where you purchased the book?
It doesn't have to be long. Just a sentence or two telling what you liked about the story!

Receive a FREE ebook and get updates when new Wild Heart books release: https://wildheartbooks.org/newsletter

BOOKS IN THE
TEXAS RANGER SERIES

Lone Star Ranger (Texas Ranger Series, book 1)

Ranger to the Rescue (Texas Ranger Series, book 2)

Lassoed by the Lawman (Texas Ranger Series, book 3)

ABOUT THE AUTHOR

This is the place where **Renae Brumbaugh Green** is supposed to provide impressive things for you to read. But since the most impressive thing about her is the fact that she almost won a car in one of those little fast-food scratch-off games one time, years ago, but she didn't actually scratch off the car until she found the card in her desk drawer, long after the deadline had passed, there's not much to say.

But if you really want to know about her writing stuff—she's the author of many books, made the ECPA Bestseller list twice, and has contributed to many more books. She's written hundreds of articles for national publications and has won awards for her humor.

She's married to a real hunk, and she's a mom to some amazing kids. She writes music, sings, and likes to perform on stage. She's a sometimes schoolteacher, a part-time chicken farmer, and an all-the-time wannabe superhero. Her favorite color is blue, unless you're talking about nail polish, in which case her favorite color is Bubblegum Pink.

If you want to know more or you'd like to read more of her books, you can find her at www.RenaeBrumbaugh.com.

ALSO BY RENAE BRUMBAUGH GREEN

Legacy of Honor (The Stratton Legacy, book 1)

If you love historical romance, check out the other Wild Heart books!

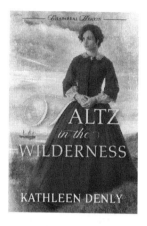

Waltz in the Wilderness by Kathleen Denly

She's desperate to find her missing father. His conscience demands he risk all to help.

Eliza Brooks is haunted by her role in her mother's death, so she'll do anything to find her missing pa—even if it means sneaking aboard a southbound ship. When those meant to protect her abandon and betray her instead, a family friend's unexpected assistance is a blessing she can't refuse.

Daniel Clarke came to California to make his fortune, and a stable job as a San Francisco carpenter has earned him more than most have scraped from the local goldfields. But it's been four years since he left Massachusetts and his fiancé is impatient for his return. Bound for home at last, Daniel Clarke finds his heart and plans challenged by a tenacious young woman with haunted eyes. Though every word he utters seems to offend her, he is determined to see her safely returned to her father. Even if that means risking his fragile engagement.

When disaster befalls them in the remote wilderness of the Southern California mountains, true feelings are revealed, and both must face heart-rending decisions. But how to decide when every choice before them leads to someone getting hurt?

~

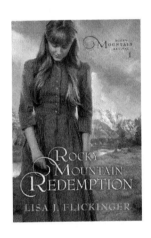

Rocky Mountain Redemption by Lisa J. Flickinger

A Rocky Mountain logging camp may be just the place to find herself.

To escape the devastation caused by the breaking of her wedding engagement, Isabelle Franklin joins her aunt in the Rocky Mountains to feed a camp of lumberjacks cutting on the slopes of Cougar Ridge. If only she could out run the lingering nightmares.

Charles Bailey, camp foreman and Stony Creek's itinerant pastor, develops a reputation to match his new nickname — Preach. However, an inner battle ensues when the details of his rough history threaten to overcome the beliefs of his young faith.

Amid the hazards of camp life, the unlikely friendship growing between the two surprises Isabelle. She's drawn to Preach's brute strength and gentle nature as he leads the ragtag crew toiling for Pollitt's Lumber. But when the ghosts from her past return to haunt her, the choices she will make change the course of her life forever—and that of the man she's come to love.

~

Marisol ~ Spanish Rose by Elva Cobb Martin

Escaping to the New World is her only option...Rescuing her will wrap the chains of the Inquisition around his neck.

Marisol Valentin flees Spain after murdering the nobleman who molested her. She ends up for sale on the indentured servants' block at Charles Town harbor—dirty, angry, and with child. Her hopes are shattered, but she must find a refuge for herself and the child she carries. Can this new land offer her the grace, love, and security she craves? Or must she escape again to her only living relative in Cartagena?

Captain Ethan Becket, once a Charles Town minister, now sails the seas as a privateer, grieving his deceased wife. But when he takes captive a ship full of indentured servants, he's intrigued by the woman whose manners seem much more refined than the average Spanish serving girl. Perfect to become governess for his young son. But when he sets out on a quest to find his captured sister, said to be in Cartagena, little does he expect his new Spanish governess to stow away on his ship with her six-month-old son. Yet her offer of help to free his sister is too tempting to pass up. And her beauty, both inside and out, is too attractive for his heart to protect itself against—until he learns she is a wanted murderess.

As their paths intertwine on a journey filled with danger, intrigue, and romance, only love and the grace of God can overcome the past and ignite a new beginning for Marisol and Ethan.

Made in the USA
Coppell, TX
07 May 2021

55253519R00103